SHADOW PHOENIX

Volume I

EPISODES 5-8

MJ MOORES

Infinite Pathways
PRESS

Shadow Phoenix: Volume 1, Episodes 5-8

Copyright © Melissa J. Moores, 2020

Published by Infinite Pathways Press 2020
P.O. Box 4, Caledon Village, ON Canada L7K 3L3

ISBN 978-1-988044-28-6
eISBN 978-1-988044-22-4

Illustrations by Ismail Mckenzie

10 9 8 7 6 5 4 3 2 1

Also by MJ Moores

The CHRONICLES of XANNIA
Time's Tempest
Cadence of Consequences
Rebels Rein
Forgotten Fallacy

D.E.M.ON. TALES
Assassin Eco-Corpses
Bobcat Got Your Tongue?
A Craptacular Understatement
Double-Dog Dare Ya

FLAWED ATTRACTION ROMANCES
Redline Drift
Final Year
Vice Ride

SHADOW PHOENIX VOL I
Episodes 1-4
Episodes 5-8

Acknowledgements

A lot goes into the making of any book and I certainly wouldn't be where I am today without my amazing editor, my writing partner, beta readers, and personal cheerleaders (you know who you are).

In particular, though, I'd like to thank Dr. Sean Palmer for his help with all things monarchy, Sensei Michael of Kushindokai Karate & Family Fitness for his insights and demonstrations on self-defence, and Chris Warrilow and Charles Barker for helping brainstorm weapons and ammo. Also, a huge thank you to my illustrator, Ismail Mckenzie, for bringing Louisa's sketches to life.

Thank you,

MJ

A New Steampunk Serial

These are the second four installments of eight short-story-length episodes that link together to form a complete novel or volume. As Charles Dickens once wrote in batches of chapters for the local paper, this story will be revealed similarly via episodes.

Each "short read" is intended to have both a general conclusion to the immediate story line, and a through-story that links each one to a larger, over-arching, plot.

It is my hope that readers who prefer shorter pieces, or who only have a limited time to read, will feel satisfied with each separate episode while looking forward to the next installment.

Happy reading.

Sincerely,
MJ Moores

EPISODE V

Lairs, Caves & Credenzas

Chapter I

Wash, Rinse, Repeat ...

The crisp night air flowed white from Louisa's lips with every exhale. A breeze tossed her long, thick curls about as she set her sights on the first target undulating in the wan moonlight.

"An' go," Joe rasped from his vantage point behind her.

She raised the Phoenix, a modified blunderbuss courtesy of Ryn, the princess-engineer. Aligning her gaze along the flared barrel, Louisa squeezed the trigger. The mini musket recoiled belching smoke and flame from the muzzle. A dull *ping* announced "target hit." Her heart no longer fluttered at the sound. She always hit that one.

Louisa sprinted across the field, dove behind a bush housing a three-tiered equestrian jump, turned, and shot at the next tin can mounted on a stake in the water hazard. She didn't wait for confirmation, just tumbled into a side-roll. Dampness from the grass clung to her training uniform—the Shadow Phoenix attire minus the dress and long coat.

She jumped to her feet, twirled, and shot at the next target from memory. Clouds blocked the faint sliver of new moon above, and mist shrouded the already darkened course. Dim orbs of lantern light glowed near the barns and the road. Cold sweat dewing her brow, she dodged invisible scorches of flame and claw-like daggers as Louisa moved around the training field. She addressed each shadow within an instant and reacted appropriately, either shooting or holding back as the situation demanded. Louisa loaded and reloaded her dragon-like pistol with the wax balls Ryn had given her for target practice.

Joe worked with her all night on building a rhythm, learning the feel of the gun and its peculiarities. The most important lesson remained loading on the move—well, that and hitting her target.

Louisa fired the last shot and collapsed to her knees. The pistol radiated heat, sending trails of smoke into the early October night. She wasn't out of breath, just finally able to breathe deeply. *Short controlled breaths* became Joe's mantra during exercises; she always thought it was to keep her from holding her breath and passing out, but now it dawned on her that her muscles were less tired and she could do longer training stints.

"Not bad, but not great," Joe said materializing from the dark to stand beside her. He leaned heavily on his walking stick, acquired from somewhere on the grounds.

"How many did I hit?" she asked.

"More 'n ya missed. Go again."

Louisa stood and removed two slugs from the leather work pouch strapped to her hips. "This is it. I'm out of ammo."

"Then let's not waste 'em. Run it backward. Target numbah seven an' four." After training together for nearly three weeks, his southern drawl no longer confused her — the rolling Rs and soft pronunciation helped focus her intent.

She nodded and moved into position. Her chest

3

ached. She swallowed hard, pushing down the worry that she'd never get this. Taking aim while standing still was hard enough, but moving and landing her mark was nigh on impossible. Joe never told her exactly how many hits she made. At least the last two runs had been *more 'n she missed*. Still, that didn't bode well, and now she was out of wax bearings.

Louisa couldn't visit Ryn tonight to request more; it was too late. Besides, she'd promised to bring supplies next time. Ryn's father had been asking questions. The last thing either woman needed was to get caught working with the other.

She inhaled deeply, raised her gun, and sighted the first target. Her arms shaking, her muscles burning, she mentally prepared herself to take the course in reverse.

"An' go."

Sweat soaked into her leather mask. With no "ping" to even remotely hint at her progress, Louisa reversed through the track, firing the bearings at target seven and four. But even then, she heard nothing. Her ire grew. They'd been at this for nearly two hours. *I'm the worst shot in the world.*

Rolling out of a forward tumble and pretending to fire at the last target, Louisa growled at the unhelpful silence. She snatched a lightning orb from her pouch and threw it into the black void. A tinny crack and an explosion of electricity lit the field.

"Guess ya knew where dat one waz," Joe drawled.

Louisa chucked the pistol to the ground. "It's useless. I've plateaued. I'm not getting any better." She pulled her hair at her temples.

"You jus' need time. Each gun's peculiar. Each person, too. Collect yah weapon an' take flight for the night."

Yeah, she needed to blow off steam. Louisa shoved the pistol into the clip holster attached to her leather belt. It smoked at her side as she headed out into the night on patrol.

Chapter II

Big Mouth Syndrome

Louisa tallied the last figure before double-checking her calculations. Escaped tendrils of hair curled across her forehead and down either side of her face. Her once strict bun slumped against the nape of her neck, and it wasn't even noon yet. Her back spasmed. She placed her pencil along the inner spine of the ledger and sat up straight on the stool next to Bennett's expansive desk.

She rotated sore joints and flexed achy muscles, hands clasped before her, hoping Bennett didn't look up. He sat hunched over flight plans and official documents. An unfinished list of invites grew ever longer. It migrated across his desk every hour or so when he made changes, put it away, then drew it out again to add other names. His brow furrowed each time he scribbled more words on the page.

Louisa reached for her teacup, which rested on one of the only empty spaces on the desk. It clattered as her hand shook, the fatigue of last night's training betraying her. Bennett sat up and tossed his pen onto the page; ink from the nub pooled slightly, but he ignored it and reached for his own tea. They sipped together. He spat his back into the cup and made a face.

"Blech, cold tea."

Louisa swallowed. She didn't mind, but he was right: ginger root, nettle, and raspberry tasted better warm. Louisa smiled, her lips still on the edge of the china cup. Isabel, the cook, had taken one look at Louisa this morning and clucked her tongue. The matronly servant knew Louisa "hadn't been sleeping well" these days. The tea helped combat fatigue, but she was certain Bennett grew tired of the flavor. Still, he never asked Isabel to change it.

"I say, this is impossible. How are you making out, Lou?"

Her insides warmed even as she swallowed another mouthful of cold tea. Heat flushed up the sides of her neck to her cheeks. She still wasn't used to the way he casually tossed about her first name. She set her cup aside and turned the ledger to face him.

"I believe, in order to cover the largest area with the fewest airships, your budget will allow for six Minis to be airborne for thirty minutes. Each ship would require four batches of two hundred orbs with a solo pilot and no crew."

"So, we'd need eight hundred … times six … Forty-eight hundred dispersal orbs." He blanched and met her gaze.

Tension squeezed her chest. Her calculations were correct, but something wasn't right.

"And we'll have enough money in the budget for that many orbs?" he asked.

"Yes, but we won't be able to hire anyone to help. I'd have to enlist the resources you already have and spend the next two-and-a-half weeks strictly making orbs."

"Wouldn't an assembly line be more efficient?" He leaned forward, abandoning his tea to search through the papers before him.

"Certainly, but if we do that, we'll need to transfer nearly half the funds from the Mini fleet to production costs. The demonstration might suffer."

He sighed and ran his hand over his dark hair. The rumpled look brought out his boyish charm. Her heart gave a little leap.

"Right, can't have that with the Queen attending. I'm certain she'll be there. What would you need? It isn't fair to ask you to come in early and stay late for fourteen days."

"Sixteen."

"No, fourteen. I won't ask you to come in on your days off. And really, we can't count tomorrow as a full day since you'll need time to train the staff and run errands. Realistically, I think we have ten days."

"I'll need three *skilled* helpers, and it'll take time for anyone to become proficient. Then, we'll need the space to work. One table is sufficient for one worker, maybe two."

He waved off her concern. "I can make that happen. Who from the staff would work well?" He met her gaze.

Louisa swallowed. As much as she'd love to steal just Isabel and Marion away from their jobs, Bennett needed them to keep his household running.

"All of them," she whispered, unsure of her place in making the request.

"All? Even Courtright?"

Louisa nodded. "I can't take four people away from their duties for two whole weeks. Everyone would have to help in shifts. Even then, there's no guarantee one or more of them won't, um … find the task as challenging as you do."

A darkness altered Bennett's features as the weight of her words sank in. Even with all the money his backers had provided after the second cloud-seeding test, the financial burden of a breakthrough weighed down the scales.

He blinked rapidly and frowned in concentration. Louisa leaned forward, arms on the desk, ready to grasp his hands — wanting to alleviate his burden. She stopped short and instead turned the notes he'd been working on to face her. She peered down at the missive to give him time to grapple with the situation without her staring. His bold cursive flowed across the page:

> Dear Majesty, *(oh no…)*
>
> You are invited *(is he serious?)* to the presentation and demonstration of my *(really?)* cloud-seeding project to the Society of Engineers on Saturday, November 4, 1876, at the Sky Port at four o'clock. Tea and refreshments to follow *(no, he can't be serious)*.
> Please RSVP the Bennett Estate no later than the Wednesday prior *(you have got to be kidding me)*.
>
> Your servant *(gracious, no)*,

Louisa tried not to shudder. *Oh, dear …* No wonder Bennett kept scratching out phrases and words—he couldn't address the Queen like that. Without asking, Louisa hunched over the page and re-wrote the royal invitation as proper etiquette dictated, the way her mother had taught her.

Bennett hunched over Louisa's figures doing his darndest to force the numbers to favor him. Their foreheads nearly touched as they worked. Bennett occasionally mumbled, querying about time-frames and resources. Louisa responded in kind and muttered aloud phrases for the invitation—most of which were met with positive grunts.

The air in the room vibrated with a comfortable, collaborative aura. Louisa ignored the rumbles of her constitution and paid no mind to Bennett's either.

A stern throat-clearing jolted both of them upright. "Ahum—"

Louisa's pulse skittered, her cheeks flushing. She looked over her shoulder. Courtright filled the doorway with her imposing frame and stern glare.

"Lunch is served and your guests await." She didn't leave, as most servants might. Instead, she narrowed her eyes at Louisa, whose insides curled and shrank.

What did I do? I never touched him. We were just working. I—

"Yes, thank you, Missus Courtright. We'll be down presently."

But the head housekeeper didn't take the hint. She remained perfectly still, her arms crossed, as Louisa and Bennett organized the desk, sort of, before walking to the door. Courtright stepped aside to let them pass and followed closely on Louisa's heels.

Down on the main floor, Louisa made to turn toward the hall leading to the kitchen. Courtright's towering presence invaded her personal space as Bennett grabbed Louisa's elbow and steered her into the parlor instead.

"No, you don't, Lou. This is a business lunch. That includes you."

Angry heat radiated off the housekeeper as she strode past. Now her hostility made sense. So much for Louisa's peace offering after her train excursion last week. Eating with guests just elevated Louisa's standing another notch. Bennett had done the unfathomable ... he'd made a servant his equal.

But Louisa had earned her position as his assistant. She knew in her bones this was what she was meant to do — to be. She turned into the parlor and nearly froze. The enchanting Elenore Rathburn sat on the settee, chiffon skirts primped wide, with a delicate smile to match.

"Elenore, Reginald, sorry to keep you waiting." Bennett nearly launched himself into the room, taking Miss. Rathburn's hand and kissing her knuckles. He vigorously shook hands with her brother.

Louisa entered; had she been wearing a dress, she'd have curtsied. As it was, she wiped sweaty palms on her slacks and gave a polite nod to both guests before sitting beside Bennett—leaving as much room between them on the small sofa as possible. The tiered service cart sat heavy with tea, finger sandwiches, fruit, and cakes. Bennett passed around small plates and inclined his head toward Louisa. Immediately, she picked up the teapot.

"Would you like some tea, Miss. Rathburn?"

"Please, I told you to call me Elly." She held out her cup atop her saucer.

Louisa did the same for Rathburn, then Bennett and herself. Before sitting, she chose a triangle of cucumber sandwich and a small bunch of grapes, mirroring Elenore's selections.

"Come now, Lou. Have some more. I know you're just as famished as I am." Bennett turned to the siblings. "We worked through tea this morning, and I heard her stomach rumble just as sure as I did mine." He winked, reached over, and plunked an egg salad triangle with a sliver of melon on Louisa's plate. Bennett and Reginald chuckled. Elenore smiled, her eyes kind. Louisa was starving, but Bennett's informality rattled her. He knew as well as she did that it wasn't polite to pile food on one's plate. She sat back, blushing.

"I'm so glad you could stop by today. Lou and I have been working on—" Louisa kicked his foot but jostled the occasional table nearly spilling the tea. Bennett glanced at her mid-sentence. Louisa narrowed her eyes at him, her heart hammering at the bold move, so like her mother.

"What Mr. Bennett means is that it's wonderful to see you up and about again, Mr. Rathburn. Have the constabulary discovered anything related to the"—she didn't want to be uncivilized and say *poisoning* outright—"unfortunate incident last Friday at the races?"

Bennett's cheeks pinkened as he nodded, biting into a sandwich square to hide his embarrassment. He was like a schoolboy—so excited he lost his manners.

Mr. Rathburn shared a knowing smile with Louisa and patted Elenore's knee. "Yes, if it hadn't been for Elly, I don't think I would've pulled through."

Louisa bit her lip to stifle a chuckle. It was terrible, but her mother said all men felt that way after ingesting Heartache. Time helped the poison pass through the system, not love and attention. Still, company, when you're ill, could make the difference between a lingering episode and a speedy one.

"The constabulary were not convinced anything was amiss until Elly pointed out my meal and a strange blue tinge to my potatoes."

Louisa caught the girl's appreciative gaze and smiled. They'd agreed it was best if Louisa wasn't connected to the incident, especially with the break-in and trouble surrounding the cloud-seeding project of late. At least, that's how Louisa had convinced Elenore not to say anything.

"And now?" Bennett asked, reaching for his hot tea.

"Well, they've done the best they can, but it's not like they're able to interview everyone who attended the races to see if they noticed anything amiss. They looked into Gunnings and his crew, but they were all accounted for. Still, it makes the most sense—and Elly agrees—that it's related to the debut of Collingworth's and Gunnings's engines."

"So, they're at a dead-end then?" Bennett asked.

"Yes, unfortunately."

"Same here. I think our case has gone cold. At least no one else has tried to sabotage this project."

"Curious, isn't it?" Rathburn set his empty plate on the occasional table and picked up his tea. "There's been a rash of incidents reported of late. What do you make of that fellow Tweed's assessment of the female vigilante? One moment she's the city's new hero, the next she's wanted as a suspect related to these crimes."

Louisa coughed into her tea. Bennett patted her back until she could take in a deep breath.

"Are you all right, my dear?" Rathburn asked.

She dropped her eyes, too embarrassed to respond. Louisa looked to Elenore, imploring help with her gaze.

"Likely just a stray crumb. Happens to the best of us." Elenore set her empty plate aside. "Dinner was just the right balance of refreshing and satisfying. You are very thoughtful, Andrew."

Bennett also set his plate aside and smiled at the girl. Rathburn glanced between the two, his expression a mix of confidence, pride, and a dash of protection.

Oh, bother, he means to pair them off. Gratitude warred with jealousy. Louisa's stomach tried to reject the food she'd eaten, and she still had a morsel of sandwich and a square of cake to get through. It was permissible to leave crumbs, but not that much. She swallowed, tried for a steadying breath, and managed to push air past the growing lump in her throat.

Rathburn coughed slightly. "So, Andrew, your invitation to lunch gleamed with possibility and excitement. Tell me, what is it you have up your sleeve now?"

Bennett's entire frame simultaneously relaxed and twitched with eagerness. "We officially have a date for the presentation of the patent. Saturday, November four. With funds from my backers, I can hire a dispersal team of six Minis."

"That's fantastic news, ol' boy." Rathburn

reached over and clapped Bennett on the shoulder.

"And I wanted to offer you the opportunity to lead the sky team for the demonstration. The Society has hinted that the Queen might even come to see it rain." A giddy boyishness took over Bennett's entire being. He couldn't sit still.

"That's incredible, Andrew!" Elenore leaned forward and clasped her hands with joy as she gazed adoringly at him.

"Yes, quite." A frown marred Rathburn's normally clear visage. "But I do believe I'll be out of town at the Edinburgh Races, showing off Collingworth's engine on the circuit until the tenth. It grieves me to have to decline the offer, but he did hire me first. It would be—"

"Yes, quite all right, Reggie. I completely understand." Bennett's tone contradicted his words. "I'll set my nose to the task of sniffing out another aeronautics expert to—"

It was Louisa's turn to clear her throat. "Excuse me for interrupting, gentlemen." *What are you doing, child?* Louisa's mother admonished in her head. Business was not normally women's concern, but she was Bennett's assistant and that meant she was just as much a part of this conversation as he. "I do believe we ought to consider Miss. Rath — um … Elly, here, before searching elsewhere. I know, traditionally, an elite representative of the community aids in the presentation of working patents to the Society. Consider Elly's recent win on behalf of her brother at the Battersea Park Races. Would it not stand to reason that her latest efforts, combined with the renown of Mr. Rathburn, might bring welcome prestige to the presentation along with the trust that comes of a forged friendship — especially now when the constabulary have abandoned our cause and with trust being such a rare commodity?"

No one spoke for a moment. Gazes flickered from Louisa to Elenore and back while the girl stared openly at Louisa with wide eyes. Mirrored in their depth Louisa's own emotions roiled between jubilation and fear. Elenore as pilot made perfect sense, but the longer the woman was around, the more opportunity she'd have to spend time with Bennett — and that churned Louisa's stomach more than she wanted to admit.

He'd been so kind to her this past month,

treating her with respect and an openness and familiarity she'd never experienced. Louisa couldn't afford to lose that.

Elenore turned to her brother but spoke to Bennett and Louisa. "While I appreciate your consideration, I travel with Reggie because we have no one else to set roots down with. It would be improper for me to remain here alone, unchaperoned. My place is with my brother." A thread of uncertainty and wistful pleading undermined the truth of her words.

"Why, if Reggie agrees, you could stay here. I have a guest suite down the opposite end of the hall on the second floor. Missus Courtright stays in the Nanny suite on the third floor, and Isabel lives with her husband on the lower level." Bennett took up Louisa's suggestion as if it was his own.

Pride blossomed in Louisa, radiating out. Rathburn pursed his lips in thought, but he still wasn't convinced. His sister's honor might be at stake as Bennett was an eligible bachelor.

"And Lou can stay here too. The room is large enough, and she can keep Elly company."

Louisa blanched. *What now?*

He turned to face his assistant. "It would work out perfectly, don't you think? Not only would Elly have a chaperone, but you wouldn't have to travel late in the evenings after working on the orbs. You'd be less at risk with the recent rise in crime." He looked between the three of them, his excitement infectious — at least, for the Rathburns.

"I think that's a fine idea. Elly, dear, would this be something you'd like to consider? It would mean reinforcing to the world your status as a pilot and your intent to present yourself in court as an independent woman. Is that what you want?" The pure affection radiating off the man made Louisa's heart fill her chest. He'd asked his sister, not told her. He truly respected her decision and proved himself a modern nineteenth-century gentleman.

Elenore took hold of Rathburn's hands. "Yes." She looked at Bennett. "Yes, I would be honored to act as lead pilot for the dispersal team." She faced Louisa, tears threatening to breach her eyes. "Thank you. This means the world to me."

Bollocks. What just happened here? How in blazes would Louisa be able to act as guardian to both Elenore and the city while trapped in Bennett's residence for the next three weeks?

"It's settled then. Courtright!" Bennett called for the head housekeeper. She bustled through the door in record time. "Prepare the upper suite for tomorrow. We'll be entertaining guests for the next three weeks."

Double Bollocks.

Chapter III

Out of the Frying Pan

Night wrapped its shadowy embrace around Louisa, but it was cold. So, Louisa folded the long leather driving duster around her too. Steam Landaus and traditional carriages lined the estate's half-moon drive just as they had the first time Louisa found herself here — at the foot of the Syndicate's door. Something squished underfoot. A foul odor accosted her. She gagged.

Bloody horses.

Louisa shook her foot, pulled farther back into the bushes, and dragged her boot over the dewy grass. The leaves rustled. She stilled.

Was that me?

Louisa listened carefully but only the faint strains of a waltz radiating from the manor house. Lamplight flooded the front, and tiny gas lights hung from the trees and the various vehicles, giving the place a fairyland or pixie feel. Elegant lengths of gauzy fabric fluttered about the grounds, pulling Louisa's usually vigilant gaze astray. She slipped through the dim side yard toward a soft beacon of light glowing from the contours of the blacked-out glass on the old conservatory. Louisa remained in the deeper shadows to the side, listening, before reaching a black-clad arm out. She knocked.

"Come in," said a distracted, muffled voice.

Louisa opened the door and slipped into her enemy's lair — well, his daughter's. Ryn leaned over the large dining-sized work table, wrestling with something. The hair scarf, which matched her cherry and silver saree, kept falling in front of her eyes. A fresh henna decorated her hands. Louisa shut the door, hurried over, and drew back the two lengths before they became entangled in the gears of the device.

The mechanism gave way. Ryn's arms relaxed and she set the two pieces down on the table before sniffing the air. Louisa let the scarf fall back into place. She shifted to the side, not only to give the engineer room but also to hide the lingering odor she'd brought in with her. The princess didn't thank Louisa, but she did reward her with a mischievous smile.

Louisa laughed. "You know, you might have ruined your outfit doing that."

"Perhaps, but not today. So, how is the pistol performing?"

"Better than I am, I'm afraid. I can't seem to hit a target while moving."

"How far away are you?" Ryn shifted to the opposite end of the workbench to collect a set of brass springs and several small fittings.

"Some closer, some farther. I'm out of practice ammo." Louisa dug into the pocket of her long leather duster and withdrew a cheesecloth baggie containing two large bricks of wax and set them on the table.

"Remember what I said about distance—it's not a sharp-shooter weapon. The closer you are to your target the better, and as long as the bullet hits the hottest part of the flame, it will work. This isn't a precision piece. Have fun with it."

"Fun ... right." Dancing with Bug's flames was

not Louisa's idea of a grand time. The spark-bug pyromaniac Ryn's father employed had little regard for what he scorched. "Speaking of which, it looks like you're holding quite the gala tonight. Shouldn't you be enjoying yourself instead of working? Your attire is more dazzling than usual — are you hiding from the festivities?"

"I'm not hiding. It's Diwali. I'm praying."

"Praying?"

"Yes, praying that I won't be disturbed. This is fun for me, and I can meditate on any number of important things while I'm back here working. Once I've been presented, I'm allowed to disappear. In fact, everyone prefers it. Besides, it's just another of my father's excuses to bring all the bigwigs together. It's not like he actually cares."

"Cares about what?"

"My mother. He insists on 'observing' her traditions as well as his own even though she's dead."

"My condol — "

"She died when I was four. I hardly remember the woman." Ryn's disinterested tone spoke more to her emotional detachment than anything else.

Part of Louisa wished she too could separate logic from emotion as easily as Ryn did. But the other part of her knew it wasn't healthy.

The princess pointed to a tool near Louisa and wiggled her fingers. Louisa grabbed the item and passed it to her.

"Why so glum? A lack of blanks for your gun is disheartening but not one to mope about. I'll have more bearings for you in two days once I'm done this project. Now, what's really the matter?" She held out her hand for a spring that had rolled across the table toward Louisa.

"It's nothing." Louisa wasn't sure if this was Ryn's version of being nice or if she just liked to gossip.

"Okay. Delude yourself."

"What does it matter?"

"Nothing, except that it does to you."

That was an odd thing to say for someone emotionally disconnected. Maybe she had feelings but only for stuff she deemed important. *Am I important to her?*

"I've gone and agreed to something at my day job that will help my employer, but it means I'll have a bully of a time getting out at night to help keep the city safe."

"No, that's not it. That would be annoying, but you're resourceful enough to find a work-around. What's really the matter?" Ryn never once looked at Louisa as they spoke and yet her acuity to the situation was unnerving.

"I—um … I think I might have feelings for my boss, but he's placed me in charge of a woman who clearly dotes on him … and is—"

"His equal?"

"I'm his equal."

"Are you? He's your boss, right?"

Louisa sighed. "Yes, but it's not like that. He respects my mind, my abilities. He doesn't talk down to me even though his schooling and stature are above mine."

"And this other woman is of similar pedigree to him?"

"Yes. She's a lady."

"And you are a woman. Well, if you ask me, it sounds like you need to prove something. Not only to him but yourse—" Ryn cocked her head to the side and stared at the door to the house.

Louisa followed her gaze.

The knob turned.

Muffled voices slipped between the door and its frame.

Ryn whipped around, eyes flashing, and pointed to something at Louisa's knees. Louisa dropped to the floor as the voices clarified and the door opened. Her heart launched into her throat. She flattened herself and searched for a way out. Ryn pointed again then turned her back to the room to face the intruder.

Louisa glanced over her shoulder—a small credenza sat with one door slightly ajar. *Blast.* She choked back a sob, pushed a crate aside, opened the cabinet, and took a deep breath before folding her body into the tight space. The door wouldn't close all the way. A three-inch gap left her vulnerable, but she didn't care. The wooden walls and ceiling breathed when she breathed, moving in and out but always drawing closer. She squeezed her knees tighter and held her breath.

"Brynna, my dear, you didn't stay at the festivities long."

"You know how I feel about being on display,"

the princess's voice deadpanned.

A second pair of highly polished wing-toed shoes joined the white slacks of the Judge. The complimenting maroon attire drew Louisa's gaze closer to the crack. The warped walls quieted enough to let her concentrate.

"Yes, and the less ruffled you are the better." His tone implied more than just the standard need to placate one's female heirs.

I knew it. There is *something different about her.*

The steward cleared his throat, prompting the Judge.

"Yes, yes, I know I need to get back. Ryn, be a dear. I need a new weapon."

"Oh?" The princess's voice perked up. He played to her weakness.

"Something that will disrupt a Wentworth mechanism. And not just the simple stuff for windows. The disrupter should have several settings, including kill. Are you up to the challenge?"

Louisa shifted. The muscles between her shoulder blades pressed against something hard and thin. She shifted but the confined space left no room to maneuver. Louisa's knee clipped the credenza's door. It swung out just as Ryn's device clattered to the floor. The engineer shifted between the men and Louisa, blocking their view.

"Clumsy me." Ryn crouched on the far side of the table and shot daggers at the dark crack through which Louisa stared.

Ryn collected the main device and several pieces that had detached on impact. The mauve-clad steward kneeled down and retrieved a cog near his shoe. The man's hooked nose and piercing coal-fire gaze locked onto the slightly open credenza. Ryn stood. He sniffed, looking around before rising.

"It seems you might have a rat infestation," came the steward's dry, imperious voice.

"What's that now?" the Judge asked, his feet shifting toward the man ... closer to Louisa. Fear ignited every nerve adding to her already roiling stomach.

"I do not have rats." Ryn's cold tone frosted the air, sending a chill up Louisa's spine. The venom lacing her words sent off alarm bells. Sure, they'd had words before, but Louisa had never seen her like this.

The steward's feet drew closer to Louisa's hiding spot. She tried to squeeze into a tighter ball, forcing her back into the sharp metal, fighting to keep from screaming. *Dear God ... not like this. Not like this.*

She tried to swallow past the dry lump in her throat, tensing every muscle, readying her body for the last stand, for freedom. Ryn's delicate red slippers trimmed in silver slid around the corner of the table and pivoted to face the steward's heels.

"If you so much as breathe on anything in my private workspace"—the air rent with ice-flamed words—"I'll cut your hands off myself and mount them above the door as a warning. You are here as a courtesy to my father. I don't take kindly to insults or trespassers. Leave."

Heavy metal slid over the table, grinding and clattering. The sharp ring of two pieces connecting punctuated the air.

"That's quite enough now, Brynna. McEvoy, stand down. I know you mean well, but my daughter is possessive of her space, and likely her feminine sensibilities have overruled logic. As for the weapon, my dear, I hope three days is challenge enough for you. Goodnight." Heavy footsteps tromped away followed by the slick slide-slap of the wing-toed shoes.

Louisa's lungs burned. Pain jolted through her but she dared not breathe, dared not move. A metallic clunk followed a rattle across the table startling a gasp from her. The too-warm air contradicted the frost of the exchange. Still, Louisa dared not move. Not just because it was prudent to wait and be certain the Judge did not return but also to avoid fracturing Ryn's space while the girl remained volatile.

The princess's tone belied an emotional reaction under its icy exterior and not because of Louisa. Boarding school mates might cause a diversion like she had, dropping the device Ryn had been working on, but something or some*one* in the exchange had triggered a deeper hatred in the girl.

Louisa remained within the confines of the credenza for a good ten minutes before clawing her way out, ignoring her sore body and her fevered mind. She slipped out the door while Ryn's back was turned. Louisa determined to keep the peace between them … and not lose her hands.

Chapter IV

Insert Foot into Mouth

The early morning sun pierced through the workshop window. Louisa squinted and peered over Henry's shoulder as he added more glass filaments to the dispersal orb. The houseman might have been good with his hands for fixing things, but creating china-thin spheres did not come naturally. Louisa glanced at Isabel, who layered her orb with a crepe of filaments. She smiled at the cook. Louisa could always count on her, no matter the situation.

Her concentration drifted as she replayed the Judge's words from last night in her mind yet again. *I need a weapon … something that will disturb a Wentworth … should have several settings … three days …*

"Oh bother," Henry muttered.

Louisa blinked and was back in Bennett's workshop, not Ryn's. Henry's third orb had gone from promising to puddle. She sighed and removed the mess from his hands. They couldn't afford to waste any more materials training him.

"Go wash up," she whispered.

"So sorry, Miss. It's just a wee bit too delicate for me." He hurried over to the dry sink. Louisa discarded his attempt before joining him. He passed her the towel, then turned to leave.

"Not so fast, sir."

Henry looked back, a rosy blush staining his cheeks.

"Come over to the table. I've another task I'm sure you can handle just fine. Sit."

He did.

Louisa hooked a stray curl behind her ear and lifted a small padded box of completed orbs onto the far end of the long workbench. She placed a list of ingredients before him. He looked at her quizzically. She gave him a tired smile and measuring spoons.

"What's this now?" he asked.

"If you can't make the orbs, perhaps you can fill them. Here." As Louisa demonstrated, she turned each dish and container so the label stood prominent for him to read. "Now, you try."

Slowly, he mimicked Louisa and followed the instructions, capping the orb with a small cork.

"Very good. Again," she encouraged. But her gaze glazed over, and she stared through the table rather than at it. *Wentworth devices are rare and expensive – used in high security. What will be available in three days that would require so much protection? Where in the city would these devices be installed? Why three days? Maybe I'm wrong, and it's not "available" in three days but will be revealed or transported soon, and the Judge needs it gone before it can interrupt or affect his business?*

"Lou!" Bennett's voice broke through her musings.

"Oh, yes, sir?" She left Henry and Isabel and hurried over to her master's — uh … employer's — desk. He searched for something under one of the many piles. Louisa longed to organize it all for him, as she had done for his notes after the fire, but she knew his desk would be like this again in less than a day. He found what he hunted for and placed it over the ledger before him.

"It looks like everything is going well," he said.

"Yes, Isabel and Henry complement each other. It's too bad we'll lose her in an hour to prep for lunch."

"I have confidence Courtright will be just as great an asset. She's never let me down. But here's the thing: I've got a meeting scheduled in an hour, and I won't be able to make it—I need to get this ledger in order for my presentation to the backers after dinner tonight."

"The meeting to request more funding?"

"The very one. Arnold and Nathan will be coming by, and I need to be ready."

"The gentlemen who got help for Mr. Rathburn at the races? The Minister for Agriculture and the plant engineer?"

"Yes, well, he's more than that. He's coming on behalf of the Royal Botanical Gardens. Nathan is on the Board of Governors, and if we can solidify long-term funding from both of them, we'll be able to open a small factory shortly after our presentation to the Society of Engineers. The Queen will want this drought to end, and we'll need to make sure another doesn't happen. An influx of money from the Crown will only take us so far; I need to plan for the long haul. Preventive measures and all."

His eyes lit up when he spoke of his design benefiting England for many years to come — that and pleasing the Queen.

"You know how important it is we do this thing right," he said.

"Yes, we discussed it in detail last night."

"Exactly. Well, the documentation needs to be done flawlessly and by someone we trust."

"Of course."

"Can you go to the meeting for me and work out the details so I can concentrate on this?" He waved at his desk.

"Um, certainly. But if I'm not here to train the staff during their scheduled shifts — "

"No problem, Lou. Isabel and Henry can train Courtright before their shift ends."

"But if Missus Courtright isn't able to — "

"She'll be fine, trust me. Can I count on you?"

Louisa blinked rapidly. She wasn't used to someone talking over her so frequently. Either she remained silent or decorum reined. But things with

Bennett had always seemed more familiar. She shook off her unease.

"Yes, sir." It meant another late night working on the orbs before she could track Morrie down and figure out what the Judge was planning, but it had to be done.

"Great. Widow Abernathy's loaned the use of her landau until the evening of the presentation. Pop over" — he scribbled a note for the older matron and handed it to Louisa — "and request to take it to London. After you meet with Tweed and convince him to work with us, come back and pick up where you left off."

"Tweed, sir?" she asked accepting the note, her insides recoiling.

"Yes, that reporter who's always at the tests. Favors us over Sterling and isn't afraid to write his opinion. Get him on board for the presentation for me. We need as many allies as we can get."

Louisa gulped and nodded before turning to leave. It was bad enough having run into Morrie at the races and then riding with him on his way back to London; now, she had to represent Bennett at a formal meeting with him … as herself. *There's no way this ends well.* Louisa *chasséd* double-time from the second floor to the basement, grabbed her wool frock, and burst out the servant's entrance just as a steam landau pulled up before the Abernathy residence.

She hesitated.

Clearly, now was not a good time to ask to use the widow's vehicle. Abernathy's driver got out and moved around to open the door for the older woman, but she caught sight of Louisa and waved, motioning the girl over. Louisa tucked the note deep into her pocket and approached.

"How are you doing, my dear?" the widow asked, a cheery smile brightening the over-cast day. Louisa noted that if the clouds in the high ceiling held any water, they kept it hidden away — the drought continued into its fifth month.

"I am well, thank you. And yourself?"

"Tickled pink, actually. My great-niece and nephew will be staying with me as their parents tour the new world for a year. It will be wonderful having children liven up the house again. Oh, there's so much to do! They'll be arriving on the train shortly. So much fuss necessary to get settled, but then the fun will begin. Oh, here." She reached into a large carpetbag, the matching wide-brimmed hat hiding her actions from view. "Could you give this to Andrew for me? He said he'd quite run out when we spoke the other day." She handed Louisa a sealed jar of jelly.

"Certainly. It's his favorite, I hear." As Louisa reached for the jar, pulling her hand from the depths of her pocket, Bennett's note fluttered free. The widow caught it before it reached the ground and took notice of the salutation.

"For me?" she asked.

"Yes, ma'am, but I see how busy you are. I can—"

"Nonsense. I can't bring you to London, but you could ride with me to Clapham Station."

Louisa opened her mouth to protest but changed her mind. "That is most generous of you. As long as I won't hinder your plans."

"Not at all. Come along, come along." She maneuvered her plump body into the landau and waved the girl in after her. Louisa obeyed and sat down across from the widow, storing the jar in her coat pocket as she did.

"Now, tell me all about what you and Andrew are planning for that patent celebration."

Louisa wasn't one to gossip, but she did reveal a few details she'd heard Bennett discuss publicly.

A short while later, they arrived at the station. Louisa departed as two rambunctious children raced across the platform and jumped into the widow's waiting arms. Again, Louisa faced the option of hiring a Steamie or taking the train. Bennett assumed she'd be out all morning and most of the afternoon if she used the widow's landau. By taking the train, in the time she saved, she could visit her mother a few days early and make sure she'd started eating—keeping Louisa's weekend open for helping Bennett with more orbs.

Knowing she planned on a personal side-trip, Louisa didn't mind using her own money to pay for a ticket to London. The only thing she minded was knowing she had to visit the reporter first, and not as the Phoenix.

* * *

The poised but chatty receptionist, who wanted to be a reporter, clacked her heels on the wood floor

45

as she led Louisa to one of the rooms along the back of the newsroom scrum. Typewriter keys clicked in opposition to the woman's measured walk and perfect stature. Louisa pulled her shoulders back a little farther. Working hunched over a table day after day had done nothing for her posture. Her mother would not approve.

"Wait here," the receptionist said and swooped back toward her station. Louisa sat in the chair on one side of a thin table in a closet of a room, the door open. She adjusted her vest and smoothed out her slacks under an open wool coat, fighting the impulse to run back out of the building. Tension kept her back stiff and straight as she reminded herself for the fiftieth time to speak with a soft, low voice.

The door shut.

Her heart jumped.

Louisa looked up. Morrie turned toward the room, unbuttoning his Norfolk jacket. He smiled at her. Not that fake reporter one he and all the rest of them had perfected, and not the sad, pained smile he reserved for Shadow Phoenix. Merriment crinkled the corners of his eyes.

"Well, you certainly aren't the gentleman I expected to see at this quarter-hour. How are you, Miss. Wicker?" He pulled the opposite chair out and sat with a jaunty hike of his leg across one knee.

"I'm well, thank you, Mr. Tweed. At least you didn't mistake me for a man this time," she quipped, having second thoughts the moment the words left her mouth.

He chuckled. "Yes, I do apologize for my assumption at the races. I didn't mean to imply any lack of femininity. I should have observed the group more closely before speaking. But that's all under the rug now, eh? And where might the man of the hour be? His telegram sounded urgent."

"He asked me to come in his stead. I hope you don't mind. Plans for the presentation of the patent have quite overwhelmed him." She couldn't admit to Bennett putting Tweed off for a more important meeting. That would not help her win the coming appeal.

"Of that I have no doubt. Sterling's second test did not go as well as Bennett's, and the Queen is calling for a solution to the drought. Bennett is in the perfect position to make history."

"He would, of course, beam at the compliment. Thank you for your kind words." Louisa hadn't had to put on airs like this when they rode to Southwark together. Something about the newspaper office and the nature of her mission set the level of formality higher than expected. Louisa channeled all of her mother's teachings from her childhood and presented herself as a lady—even though she worked for a living. Heat crept up to her exposed ears above her frock coat as she tucked away a stray lock of hair.

Morrie popped up from his chair. "Where are my manners? Here, let me help you." He bustled around and lightly plucked her wool coat from her shoulder. He laid it across one end of the skinny table before resuming his former position.

"Now, how may I be of service to you?"

"Mr. Tweed, Mr. Bennett wants me to extend to you first rights for documenting the patent presentation before the Society of Engineers and, potentially, as you pointed out, the Queen."

His eyes widened in surprise. She carried on, not letting him get a word in edge-wise.

"You see, Mr. Bennett quite approves of your

reporting style, and he'd like to hire you to take the official photographs and make the third-party unbiased report of events at the presentation. In no way does he want to influence your job to report on the event for the paper, but neither does he trust just anyone to handle this delicate and momentous task. Will you accept?" Excitement raised her voice a bit at the end. She worried he might detect something in her tone, but he flashed her another dazzling smile, his loose sandy-blond curls bobbing in time to his nod. An electrified jolt ignited her.

"My goodness, this is an unexpected honor. I'll have to confirm with my manager to make sure there's no conflict of interest, but I'd love to help. Only the Society of Engineers and the Queen's staff will see the official report, correct?"

"And Mr. Bennett, but yes, that's right."

"So, the only public version of events would be what I choose to write on behalf of The Chronicle?"

"Mmhm. That is our understanding as well."

He leaned forward and clasped her hands. Louisa's heart rate spiked. Had she been a lady of delicate constitution she might have swooned.

Maybe she did a little anyway. He looked so happy for a change. She did that. *My news did that.* Still, she'd never seen his gray eyes sparkle so keenly before—well, maybe that one time when she'd accused him of abandoning her. No, abandoning Phoenix. But that had been more of a fire than a sparkle.

"Let me confirm for you. Be right back." And he rushed from the little room so fast he might never have been there at all except for leaving the light woodsy hint of his cologne behind.

She checked her pocket watch after fifteen minutes and pressed her lips together. *Maybe there's an issue with his boss.* Louisa let her shoulders droop and slouched into the wooden chair, crossing her legs and folding her hands on her lap. Her arms twitched. She tried to keep still. Louisa stared at the ceiling as the Judge's word filtered through her thoughts. *Variable setting, including kill ... three days ... three days ...* She slammed her hands on the table and stood up. Morrie needed to know, but she couldn't give up her cover. *Which Wentworth? What is he up to? I have all the clues but —* "Dammit!"

"Everything all right?"

Louisa whirled around. Morrie turned to wave at someone before re-entering.

"Yes, everything's fine," she said in her low, soft tone and offered him a polite smile, clasping her hands behind her back and squeezing them tight.

"Oh." He glanced over his shoulder. "I guess I heard someone in the next room."

She raised her eyebrows, playing into her apparent innocence.

He chuckled, then beamed his brilliant smile at her, melting away all the nervous energy, warming Louisa from her toes to her cheeks. "Never mind. I have good news."

* * *

Louisa tucked the bag of Queen's Approved butterscotch bites into the pocket opposite Bennett's jar of crabapple jelly and hailed a Steamie to Southwark. The steam clock in front of the newspaper office blasted the hour as she climbed into the waiting vehicle. Louisa hadn't brought a meal with her, but perhaps she could pick up a meat pie from a street vendor on her way back to

Bennett's.

A small smile kept tugging at her lips on the drive. It didn't matter that she knew her destination was the asylum she'd abandoned her mother to nearly eight months ago. Nor did it bother her so much that she had to wait until that evening to speak with Morrie as Phoenix — because she'd get to see him again.

Stop it, Louisa. Don't be so foolish. But even after another internal reprimand, her lips tugged up again.

The moment she stepped from the Steamie and paid her fair, though, Louisa's expression fell. The strange jolt of happiness evaporated. An imposing gray stone manor rose before her. She forced one foot in front of the other as her brain stalled on the image of her mother's gaunt face and wheelchair-bound body. Louisa walked through one side of a double set of arched doors and over to the receiving desk. She licked her lips, stomach threatening to bring up any last traces of breakfast. She took a deep breath.

"Good day. I was wondering if I could visit with my mother briefly. Marie Pierce."

The nun-like matron behind the desk looked at the intake log. "I don't have you scheduled for a visit," she said, not looking up.

"No, I didn't have time to write ahead. I happened to be in London on business and have a few moments to stop in. I know advance notice is preferred, but I am here during visiting hours and Miss. Pierce's case is especially delicate. I'd like to check in on her, if you please." None of the soft, low tones from Louisa's earlier conversation intruded now. If that woman tried to keep Louisa from her mother —

"Yes, certainly." She dinged a bell and a male orderly, dressed in gray and dull white, shuffled in from down the hall. "Please prepare Miss. Pierce for a visitation."

The orderly nodded and left. The receptionist indicated a wooden high-backed chair set off to one side of the entrance. Louisa took the hint and sat. They left her waiting just long enough for all of her nerve to drain and pool on the floor. She stood to leave just as the same orderly reappeared and inclined his head for Louisa to follow. The man led her down the passage toward the courtyard. No one sat outside today. The inner community room vibrated with a dozen or more separate breaths, but no one spoke. The orderly nodded to an empty seat across a small table from a frail woman in a headscarf, but not just any woman.

"Mother." Louisa sat across from her, and the orderly dissolved into the gray of the walls. The woman looked up and stared at Louisa. She didn't seem any more robust than before, but then, it hadn't been a week yet. Still, Marie's gaze cut into Louisa like it had when she was a child.

"You came back."

"I said I would. Are you eating?"

She shrugged.

Louisa stood to leave. "Then you have no need of the news I promised." Her heart bubbled up into her throat at the lie. She had no news. Her mother was going to die.

"I'm managing the porridge in the morning," Marie said.

Louisa sat back down.

"A small chunk of bread with jelly and tea in the afternoons."

"That's a good start." A familiar ache speared

out from her torso. "Have you been moving around more? I don't see your wheelchair."

"Yes, I walked here from my room. Now, what's so important you wouldn't let me die in peace?"

"That was anything but peaceful and you know it." Her mind reeled. "There's a job opportunity you would be perfect for. I submitted your resume this morning." *You're lucky she never could tell when you were lying.* "I should hear by early next week if they'd like an interview. It's very respectable."

"What is it?"

Good question. "A governess position." *Says who? First rule of the Liar's Club – base everything off a grain of truth.* So far, all she'd done was talk out the side of her mouth.

"Really? Where? Whose household? Do they know who I am?" A quiver edged the restrained excitement in her mother's voice as though she dare not allow herself to believe it.

"Um …" The image of two children running into their Great Aunt's arms flooded her synapses. "Abercromby. The widow is housing her niece's little boy and girl as their parents travel abroad for a year. It'll be a great foothold to get back into legitimate work. But if she asks for an interview, I refuse to bring a half-starved rake with me or my reputation will be on the line. Promise me you'll keep eating—work up to three proper meals and tea by my next visit."

"And when will that be?"

"A week, week and a half at most. Widow Abercromby will let me know after she's done accepting applications."

"Does she know who I am? Who you are?"

I'm nobody. "No. I've given you a nom de plume—Mary Wicker. You, dear mother, are starting over. No baggage this time. Can you handle that?"

Marie Pierce wavered a moment. So much weight rested in a name. Mary Wicker was a nobody compared to who her mother really was, but at least her reputation was clean.

Louisa's mother nodded and let a small smile slip before her daughter stood to take leave. As Louisa walked away from the clingy gray shadows of the asylum, her only thought was how it might be possible to turn a complete fabrication into the truth.

Chapter V

Going Out on a Limb

The next evening, Henry set the last two pieces of luggage down just inside the large room on the second floor of Bennett's townhouse. Elenore squealed, clapped her hands, and pulled Louisa into a twirl. Henry chuckled, gave Louisa and her new roommate a tip of his cap, and disappeared back down the hall.

Elenore released Louisa's hands and tumbled onto her bed. "Oh, joy! It's official. The last of your things have arrived. Can you believe it?" she gushed before spreading out her skirts and nesting in the center of the bed.

Louisa grabbed the handle on the two cases and lifted them across to the double wardrobe on her side of the spacious room, then returned and locked the door. She twitched the curtains closed on the large window between their beds. Few stars lit the darkening sky above the postage-sized backyard, but it was early yet — for her, anyway.

Her roommate shifted from the bed to the dressing screen in front of her wardrobe and systematically removed layers of clothing. Louisa lifted a satchel from the top of one bag and set it at the end of her bed before opening her wardrobe and organizing the clothes.

"I still can't believe Reggie agreed to let me stay. I saw it in his eyes — he wasn't going to until Andrew suggested we room together," Elenore said from behind the screen.

"I noticed that too. I'm glad I could be of help. This is a big step forward in your career. Do you suppose this is what you were meant to do? Be a pilot?"

"I don't know. Until we raced together last week, it was a curiosity. A hobby. But being in charge like that — *Zooterkins*! I simply had to do it again. Opportunities like this don't come around every day. Andrew has no idea how significant this is."

"Oh, I don't know. He might surprise you. The

way he acted like it was his ideas to bring you on was actually quite comical. I'm certain he kicked himself for not thinking of it first." And Louisa kicked herself for getting backed into a corner.

With Elenore moving in yesterday, Louisa couldn't go home to get her Phoenix gear. What few things she'd brought, as a show of good faith, would not work as alternate clothing for either crime-fighting or training. She could only hope that Joe remembered Louisa mentioning a coming restriction on her evening activities. But she had to get out tonight. Morrie still didn't know about the impending heist, and Louisa hadn't figured out where it would happen yet.

"I can't thank you enough, Lou. For the next three weeks, it'll be like having a sister."

Louisa smiled to herself as she set stationery supplies in one of the two desks flanking the door. Bennet had thought of everything. "You might come to regret that, you know. I do work every day. We're on a tight schedule. We have so many orbs to make—I'll have to return to the workshop again tonight to make more for Henry to fill in the morning. He really is all thumbs when it comes to crafting."

Elenore stepped out from behind the screen dressed in a nightgown and plaiting her hair for the night. "I can help. Put me to work. That's why I'm here. I can't abide being idle."

Louisa slung her satchel over her shoulder and toed one of the travel bags farther under the bed.

"Thank you, but I don't know how much time you'll have to help. Trust me, Bennett has plans for you. Last night's private fundraising dinner was only just the start. You, my dear, are his celebrity and he will make sure your time is filled with special teas and personal interviews."

"But as my chaperone, you'll be with me, right?"

"For many of the occasions, but Courtright will likely be with you more often. Remember, my job is to make sure we have enough orbs for the presentation. If I'm with you during the day, I am working longer hours in the evening."

"Well, I'll do what I can, when I can. Hopefully, you won't be busy every evening."

As much as she wanted to be busy, Louisa wouldn't be able to go out as often as she had been. *It's only for three weeks. Three weeks.*

"I need to get back to it now. Don't wait up. I work pretty late." Louisa unlocked the door, patted her vest pocket to check she had her key, nodded, and slipped out.

"Goodnight, Lou," Elenore called and pulled a book from her bedside table.

Louisa had to be careful. She dropped her bag behind the desk in the workshop and headed over to the readied supplies. For a good hour she worked steadily on making orbs before Bennett popped his head around the corner and advised her not to be too late. He'd done that last night, and before she moved in; that had always been her signal to pack up for a late walk home. But now, this was home—at least temporarily.

She worked for another half an hour, making sure no noises arose from either end of the house, and noted when Courtright lowered the main foyer's chandelier to snuff the lights for the night. Louisa set the two work tables up for a fresh start in the morning. She changed into her Shadow Phoenix attire in the back corner of the supply area, a tall cabinet door acting as her screen just in case someone wandered in unannounced.

Louisa nestled her day clothes under her nightdress in the bag, and she slung her boots around her neck, laces tied together. She tiptoed across to the open window behind Bennett's desk. Louisa dared not open it any wider just in case thieves took notice. So, she squeezed out the narrow opening onto the tiny brickwork ledge delineating the second floor from the first.

The house beside her stood close enough she could reach it by leaning just over an arm's length above the gap — but there were too many windows right there. She couldn't afford to tap one by accident. What Louisa really wanted was a bloody tree she should scale down, but the poor excuse for one in the backyard barely produced apples let alone was tall or near enough to be of any use.

Near the corner of the house, Louisa let her upper body fall forward toward the opposite wall. Cold brick bit into her palms, jarring her as she angled nearly forty-five degrees above solid ground. Little by little she walked first her hands then her feet down opposite walls in increments until she reached the ground. Donning her new black boots and straightening her leather mask,

Louisa set out among the shadows to Morrie's place.

* * *

"Good Lord, woman. Why do I always find you in my room?" Morrie said by way of greeting.

"This is your room?" A tightness gripped Louisa's chest. "You live here?" Suddenly, sitting on the basic cot by the wall in the small space became so much more intimate.

"Yes," he deadpanned and stood with his arms crossed, staring at her.

"But, I thought"—she looked from the wardrobe to the wooden chair back to the floor at her feet and stood up—"this was a spare room. A place where you helped people."

"I can see how you might think that as I had nowhere else to bring you that first night when Scythe fractured your ribs and Brick cracked your head against the wall." Louisa cringed, recalling the two thugs who worked for the Judge. "No, you're the only one who frequents this place other than me. Though I am working to rectify that. We missed you last night. Everything all right?"

"Yes—I mean, no. Ugh, *damnfino*. I'm fine

except that my circumstances have changed for the next while, and it'll be difficult getting out of an evening now. That being said, we have a serious problem. The Judge is planning something big."

Morrie dropped his defensive stance and approached her. "What's that now? How do you know?"

"I overheard him ordering up a new weapon from Ryn. It's something special. A disruptor of some kind that's supposed to take out a Wentworth device. And it'll have a kill setting."

"When?"

"It's supposed to be ready for tomorrow night."

"Where?"

"I don't know. That's why I opted out of training or hunting in the shadows tonight. I need your help."

Morrie nodded and paced past her, following a pre-set course worn into the wooden floor. "If the weapon is supposed to disrupt a Wentworth, it'll have to be a well-fortified location."

"That's what I thought too." Her earlier tension melted from her body as she took up an alternating pacing cycle. The two of them wove in and out, back and forth, keeping time in a strange dance.

"Bank," he said.

"Opera House," she parried.

"Patent office."

"Botanical Garden — greenhouses."

"Basilica."

"Museum."

"Crown Holdings. Wait — you might be on to something."

"Really? What?" They took a step toward each other, the air alive with ideas.

"The museum. They submitted a press release two days ago about bringing in an archeological find from one of the old Roman dig sites up north. Claimed they recovered ancient tech that's supposed to change the world." He dug into his pockets and emptied scraps of paper and small note pads onto the tiny collapsible table, sifting through them.

"Well, that would certainly catch the eye of a notorious criminal."

"If only," he muttered.

"If only, what?" Louisa stepped closer and

hovered over Morrie's shoulder, close enough to breathe in his woodsy cologne.

"If only the Judge was notorious. The problem is, only us and the bad guys know who's behind all this."

"Right. Good point. So, what exactly is worth killing for this time?" Louisa asked.

Morrie snatched up a crumpled sheet of paper, opening it for Louisa to read. Heat radiated off the reporter as she looked over his shoulder at the missive.

"No bloody way ..."

Chapter VI

Performance Issues

As always, Louisa arrived late to the crime scene. Her new roomie had wanted to talk about her day out schmoozing big-wigs with Bennett while Louisa had worked double-time to make up for Thursday's delays in the workshop.

The side staff entrance to the museum held a darker line along the doorjamb than any of the windows in the same area. No guards stood nearby or walked the perimeter. Louisa became one with the shadows and slipped closer to the entryway. Scorched wood surrounded melted metal.

Bug's been practicing with his flame launcher. The precise destruction was not his usual M.O. Still, no one else opened a door like that.

Inside, the dim light of the moon cast angular shadows across the marble floors. Louisa's chest tightened. Many a day she'd spent within these walls, learning of the wonders they held … watching her mother work a mark as Louisa studied. She blinked back the past and looked for clues. But Bug hadn't left any. Perhaps he finally learned a trick or two from his partner. Scythe was a human weapon, lean and sharp like the twin combat blades that hung crossed over her hip.

Where would they be? The artifact was due to arrive earlier that morning. Even if the curators had a display space ready in advance, they'd wait to assess the piece before announcing its authenticity and then hold a reveal gala to fundraise for the museum. None of that had yet made the news, but money did make the world go 'round.

In that case, it's likely in the vault. Thus, the need for a disruptor. A top of the line Wentworth did not rely on pins or cranks or keys—it dealt with frequencies and levers. If the Judge had access to the original patent, Ryn would have been able to make a weapon capable of neutralizing any alarm trigger … and anybody standing in the way.

Louisa headed for the back stairwell through various alcoves and display rooms. Both ancient and modern artifacts cut long, dramatic shadows across her path. She passed three unconscious guards along the way as she followed a smoky trail toward her destination. Bug had no idea the kind of damage even residue from his flame launcher could have on the artwork.

Darkness clung to the archway leading to the cellar storage and analysis rooms. The absolute-black velvet air mocked her. Louisa naturally clung to and hid in the shadows, but a smothering threat loomed within its depths. Still, she had to tear through it to reach the cutpurses.

Complete darkness enveloped Louisa, the chill air wrapping her within its cold tendrils. Razor wind swept toward her head. Louisa ducked, pushing off from the dark step and colliding with a mass. The source of the razor wind growled, then grunted as Louisa landed on her adversary at the bottom of the stairs. A dim thread of light from up the corridor crossed the grappling women.

Scythe's brown skin didn't look so smooth and perfect up close. A network of fine scars attested to either her training or rough past or maybe both. The assassin locked Louisa's head in a tight arm hold. Louisa gasped, the pressure on her throat cutting off her air. The guardian's mind went blank, and she flailed, struggling to get loose. Between the white spots flashing before her eyes came the image of Joe's dark features, two bushy gray eyebrows raised, igniting her training.

Don' be flashy. His voice melted some of the fear.

Louisa tucked her chin down, protecting her throat as she reached around Scythe's back and grabbed the assassin's arm. Scrambling up onto their knees, the women struggled as Louisa slammed her free hand into the *halfinch's* face. The impact forced the woman's head back. Louisa clawed at her adversary's nose and eyes. Scythe tensed, shifting her focus away from her arm. Louisa angled a leg behind her attacker's knees and flung the two of them backward onto the ground.

Scythe's arm straightened up over Louisa's face. The guardian's mask flipped from her nose to her forehead. The thief yanked the driving coat off Louisa as she scrambled up. She slid the backward mask down over her eyes and grabbed a lightning orb from her pouch. Louisa smashed it onto the floor and took off down the hall.

Whoa, that was close.

Rounding the corner, gasping for breath, Louisa spotted Bug standing before an iron door at the end of the dim hall. He adjusted a nob and several levers on a relatively small device shaped like a futuristic ray gun — which was exactly what it was.

The disruptor.

Morrie had looked into the patent on the Wentworth locking mechanism — particularly the operation of the release and how each device was attuned to a specific frequency. A lower resonance could be gauged, but the moment an operator went over, a backup deadbolt dropped, making the door impenetrable. If that happened, it would be easier to bust the cinderblocks holding the doorframe than doing anything of consequence to the iron encasing the mechanism.

"Stop!" Louisa pushed herself off the wall before he could find the right frequency to disengage the lock.

Bug glanced up at her and resumed his adjustments. Louisa's head was yanked back, her scalp screaming. She slammed into the wall and bit her tongue, spitting blood. Louisa grabbed her attacker's wrists and forced pressure in just the right place. The hands let go. Louisa turned.

"Scythe!"

"Surprise, chickee. Had you thrown that thing at my head, not the ground, you might have knocked me out longer. Clearly, it wasn't one of your special ones, or I doubt I'd still be breathing." The assassin leaped forward; her long blades hummed as they sliced through the air.

Louisa raised her arms and jumped back. Twin swords penetrated the sleeves of her black chemise. *Bloody hell. I still don't have any protection from those damn things.* She'd been so caught up with Bennett's deadlines and her temporary move, she hadn't had time to think about adding extra protection to her uniform. Louisa had hoped her leather coat would be enough, but it wasn't doing her any good lying on the ground at the bottom of the stairs. She had no way to protect herself.

Not true.

She dipped back, counterbalancing by stretching out a leg and bending the opposite knee.

Listening to the rhythm of her heart, Louisa twirled around her foe and punched her in the kidney before dropping *à terre*, to the ground, as Scythe slashed out. She channeled *Alegria*, the bullfighting dance, never losing sight of her opponent.

Locking onto Scythe's sharp, staccato pacing, Louisa used an alternate syncopation to fill the spaces the assassin left open—jabbing and kicking and punching whenever the thief left herself exposed. Louisa spun the woman in circles, etching away at the thief's equilibrium. But some part of Louisa's mind chided her for falling into a trap. Scythe kept her busy while Bug worked on the frequency settings. Louisa had forgotten to keep an eye on him, to be as much of a distraction to him as Scythe was to her.

The groan of a large, heavy door heralded his success.

Mafficking nonsense.

No matter how hard she tried, Louisa couldn't get the advantage. She had nothing to fight with but her body—the orbs and Phoenix pistol useless.

I need a weapon.

Oh yeah? What are you going to do with it?

"*Zounderkite*," she cursed herself.

Yer hans are weapons, Joe's words echoed through her head. They'd only done limited offensive tactics lately as she learned how to handle the gun. Still …

Scythe's blade flashed past Louisa's ear, shifting her wild curls.

Now.

Louisa grabbed the thief's exposed wrist and turned into the woman's body, avoiding the second blade. Her pulse spiked and every nerve crackled with pent up electricity. Louisa grabbed Scythe's other wrist, crossing both their arms over Louisa's chest in an awkward hug.

Scythe growled and shifted her head back. Louisa tilted to the side as the assassin's forehead met air. She snapped her head to the other side, capturing Scythe in a vice between her ear and shoulder.

"Argh! I'll eat you alive," Scythe snarled, trapped.

Louisa worked to find the pressure points on the thief's wrists. Bug sauntered out from the vault, placing a contraption into his satchel, the displacer hanging from his belt. Louisa pressed into Scythe's lower forearm and forced the assassin's grip to freeze. She linked her legs through Scythe's and wore the slight Filipino as a coat, marionetting her arms, still trapping her face. Louisa couldn't hold her long, but maybe …

"Set it down, Bug. You're not going anywhere." Louisa pointed the tips of Scythe's blades at the little man, fighting to hold the assassin against her back. Every muscle screamed at her, but this time Louisa wasn't helpless.

Bug raised his eyebrows. "Well then, Scythe, you look a little tied up. Too bad the boss likes you." He placed the bag at his feet and pulled the flame launcher from over his shoulder.

"Bloody hell," Louisa cursed.

She heaved Scythe into the wall and scrambled low, covering her head. Louisa's arms throbbed but she curled herself into a ball and drew her pistol. Flames scorched the air above her. The door on her right crackled and caught fire. She rolled past it and up onto her knees, shooting a round, extinguishing the flames. Louisa twisted and aimed down the hall, hesitating.

Her hands shook. She tried to swallow past the lump blocking her throat. Down the smoky corridor, a flash of red leather and the business end of the launcher disappeared around the corner. A layer of sweat coated Louisa's body, the heat making her mask stick to her face. The slimy layer between the leather and her skin surprised her almost as much as freezing up had. It'd never happened before.

She shook herself and jumped to her feet, racing down the hall after the thieves. Luckily, not much could catch fire down there other than the doors to more minor storage rooms. Louisa scurried after the pair, picking up her coat at the base of the stairs and covering her head with it as she rose to denser smoke above.

Damn. He must have set several fires earlier, before heading to the vault. Louisa turned toward the path leading out but stumbled over something soft.

It groaned and coughed.

Double damn!

"Argh!" she yelled, abandoning the chase and grabbing hold of the unconscious guard at her feet. As important as that ancient artifact was, lives were worth far more—and the thieves had left several other unconscious guards littered throughout the museum.

She hauled him and another man, each by one hand, across the highly polished floors, her coat over her shoulders and hooding her head to keep the smoke from choking her. Louisa deposited the men outside, but before she turned to go back into the flaming building, a broad, sinewy form hugged the shadows, chasing after Bug and Scythe.

Another minion? She didn't think so. The body's movements were too familiar.

Whistles blasted from up the street and a siren wailed. Louisa glanced into the cool night toward safety but shook her head and plunged back into the smoky furnace. She knew where the other two guards lay. If they perished, their deaths would be on her head.

Louisa collected the unconscious men and dragged them to a side window just off the atrium. She needed to avoid running smack into the constabulary on her way out. She opened the window and grappled with the dead weight of the men, levering each out of the window, hoping they didn't hit their heads as they tumbled to the ground. Louisa perched on the ledge, flung her coat back from her head, and leaped from the window to the far side of the guards.

Raised voices and hollers mingled with whistle blasts. Several firefighters with buckets raced around the front corner of the building. Louisa turned to run but staggered with the weight of a man clinging to her ankle. She tried to shake him off, but he only held tighter.

"Look! It's the Phoenix," a fireman shouted.

"*Codswallop*," she cursed and yanked an orb from her pouch. Shards grazed her knuckles, broken orbs from her fight with Scythe. She smashed the device on the ground sending out a jolt of electric energy. The blast drew more attention, but the guard let go.

She ran.

Dashing for the deepest shadows away from the museum, Louisa crashed into someone hiding there. She staggered back. Hands gripped her wrists before she could react.

"You're under arrest," the familiar, condescending voice ground out. He slapped a pair of

years meant her mother no longer bore the experience of a scorned and abandoned teenager — but the wisdom of a hardened woman.

"Stand up! All of you," she'd commanded.

They had, even Louisa. Especially Louisa.

"Come here and line yourselves up facing that wall. Now, on the count of three …"

"Run forward and back," Louisa's seventeen-year-old self said aloud and stood up in the small cave-like space. She was the only one this time, but she was twice as tall, three times as strong, and determined as hell to be free.

And she ran.

From one side to the other, Louisa flew up each wall and pressed her body into the side with all her strength and momentum. Back and forth and back until a deep sway rocked the wagon up onto the apex of two wheels.

Louisa hovered in the air, determination etched onto her features.

She held her breath.

The paddy-wagon toppled.

The door cracked and sprang open.

Louisa collapsed onto the wall-turned-floor and

scrambled out into the night, slipping between two buildings, heart pummeling her chest. She launched herself from one inky shadow to the next, some small part of her brain struggling to determine where she was and reclaim her bearings. Her breath came in bursts, her heart (a mile ahead) pulled her from one alley and lane to the next until she slammed into another living shadow.

Chapter VII

Lightning & Thunder

Louisa staggered back, holding her arms up to shield her face. A broad man covered head-to-foot in fitted brown leathers grabbed her forearms and pulled her toward him. A bone-deep ache gnashed through her arms striking up from her cuffed wrists. She gasped and shuddered.

"Phoenix, it's me. Are you all right?" The familiar baritone voice rumbled through her, warming her from her ears to her toes. He let go of her arms and clarity returned.

"Morrie?"

"Shh—no names. Are you all right?" Concern laced his tone. Something she hadn't detected since the night they'd met.

"I think so. I—Hersh—"

"Hersh?"

"Inspector Hersh. He caught me coming out of the museum. Tossed me in the wagon" — she held out her cuffed hands — "I saw — did you chase after Bug and Scythe?"

"Yes, but when you didn't follow, I got worried. The paddy-wagon, you say? How did you get out?" He turned the heavy metal surrounding her wrists up and over gingerly.

Louisa sighed and lost her equilibrium, wavering. Morrie caught her and gently turned her face to look up at him. Her eyes remained downcast. Her heart constricted. *Now he knows.* With his fingers supporting her chin, his leather-clad thumbs traced the ridge of her cheekbone. Louisa's gaze flickered up and met the multi-layered pieces of oblong glass that formed a darker central oval covering his eyes. The slight triangular extension over his nose and the multi-tonal browns and beiges flaring out from his eyebrow ridge gave him a hawk-like appearance.

His voice resonated low like thunder, "Your mask is gone."

"Hersh, again." She tugged her chin away and looked down, her wild curly locks tumbling to hide her embarrassment. "And now you know who I am. Please don't tell—"

Morrie held up a hand. "Wait. You've guarded your identity closely these past weeks—wouldn't even let me take those blasted goggles off to clean that gash on your head when we first met. Here." He caught her hands, worked a thin piece of metal into the key hole and popped the lock. The cuffs clattered to the ground between them. He brought her fingers to touch her face where her mask usually rested. "Give a rub."

She pressed into the skin and moved already slick fingers around before squinting at them.

"Black?"

"Shoe polish, I'd say. I can't see much. You look like a raccoon." Morrie moved closer.

The commotion by the museum grew louder, carrying on the crisp fall night air.

"What's that? Blood?" He pulled Louisa closer and tilted her chin up again. His warm breath caressed her cheek. Her heart hiccupped. She held her breath.

Morrie slid his free hand along the sleeve of her leather jacket, caught her laced palm, and lifted it to eye-level. The bare tips of her fingers glistened red.

"You're bleeding." His gaze searched her head to boot. "You're hurt."

"I didn't think I was." She looked at her hand and followed the trail back up under the coat sleeve. "Scythe. She must have nicked me with her swords."

"You fought her unarmed?"

"My arms worked just fine, thank you."

Morrie cocked his head to the side, pursing his full lips. She couldn't take her eyes off them. But then, the sweep of his neck led to such broad shoulders and strong arms. Arms kept hidden under layers of fabric during the day now rippled beneath the form-fitting leather suit.

Louisa blinked. *What am I thinking?* She stepped back but her head spun and she lost her balance again.

"Whoa, there. You're light-headed. Must have lost a lot of blood. Come on. We have to get you out of here."

"But—but what about the artifact? The whole reason ..." She couldn't think straight.

"Don't worry. I don't have it, but I know where it is. Come on." He wrapped an arm around her waist and nudged her forward. Louisa's legs automatically picked up the pace, and they jogged back to the tavern. By the time they arrived, Morrie mostly carried Louisa as she focused on moving her feet. He led her right past the lower-level side door.

"W-what?" She glanced back. "I don't understand."

"Remember our conversation last night? I mentioned working on something so we wouldn't be meeting in my room constantly?"

She vaguely recalled him muttering something like that. He guided her to the dead end and hoisted her up onto the brick wall attached to the rear of the building.

"Just drop down onto the patio," he said.

Louisa held her breath to steady her spinning head and slipped over the edge. Morrie followed close after, gathered Louisa to his side, and unlocked the back door to the main floor.

Where was he hiding the key? Never mind that, where had he stashed the lock pic? No pockets on that suit ... She stared at the way his muscles flexed and moved under the soft leather.

He led her into the dim building — large sheets covered furniture-like shapes as he brought her, without faltering, through the maze of rooms to the stairs at the front. Louisa tried to lift her feet to climb to the second floor, but she tripped and turned an ankle.

"Dagnabbit," she cursed. Morrie's arm tightened around her. She wanted to lean into the strong warmth of his body and fall asleep but something in the back of her mind screamed; she just couldn't make out the words ... Oh, that was it — *walk*. Louisa focused again on making it up the stairs without falling.

At the top, Morrie left her leaning against the wall. He moved through the sparsely furnished open space, lighting candles and small kerosene lamps. He picked up a larger candle with a holder, collected her from the wall, and carried her into the next chamber. The sheets draped in this room did nothing to disguise the four-poster bed against the far fall. But he didn't stop in the room filled with ghosts; Morrie took her into the loo and placed her atop a closed commode.

He kneeled before her and slipped the coat from around her shoulders. Oversized, it fell easily away from her arms. Louisa stared at the shredded fabric of her black chemise as she hid her finer facial feature behind her mass of curls. She might still be wearing a "mask" but he would recognize her if he held the light too close.

Gingerly, Morrie unclasped the pearl buttons holding the fabric tight to her wrists and guided first one hand, then the other, through the long slits in the silky material.

She shuddered. Blood coated her arms. Twin slices drew angry red lines from her inner elbows to her outer wrists. The gouges near her elbows throbbed. Morrie removed his gauntlet-like gloves and nudged the torn flesh.

Louisa gasped.

It was more than just a scratch … a lot more.

"It's okay, Phoenix. I mean, most of it's superficial. Your blood has started to clot but these areas here" — he drew a line in the air above a two-inch section near her elbows — "I'm concerned about. You've lost a lot of blood." He looked at the floor and held the backs of her hands, keeping her sliced arms face up.

"You can fix me, right?" she whispered.

He frowned and looked at her from the side before setting her hands on her knees and shoving his mask back. "Let's get you cleaned up so I can see how bad they really are."

Louisa nodded. Her eyes fluttered closed only popping open at the sound of cloth tearing. A mirror hung above a basin with a decorative faucet. *On the second floor?* Running water in a commode like this meant upper-class perks.

"Wh-where are we?" she asked.

Morrie's face appeared before her. Close. Too close? He stared first into one eye and then the other.

"Stay with me now. Let's get your arms fixed up. Do you prefer whiskey or bourbon?"

Louisa gave him a squinty-eyed look. "Neither. I don't drink. And whatever you gave me in my tea last time doesn't count."

"You need something. I can make up a salve to help numb the pain after, but I don't have any pharmaceuticals — and nothing is open right now. That leaves alcohol, and not just for disinfecting."

Louisa balked. "No. No alcohol." She shook her head. Yes, it numbed the senses but she needed to be able to get home after this—she needed to keep her wits about her. Alcohol had helped her mother "forget" but it also had helped her "loosen up" for particularly amorous clients. Louisa refused to put herself in that situation.

"This will be painful without it."

She nodded.

Morrie dunked a piece of white fabric into the sink, ringing the bulk of the water out before laying it across the hot flesh of her arm, then removing her fingerless lace gloves before wetting another piece of cloth.

She jolted.

He placed the other cloth over the opposite arm, then stood up and removed the upper half of his suit, allowing the torso and attached headpiece to hang from his hips behind him.

Louisa's eyes grew wide. She was not hallucinating. A myriad of fine white scars crisscrossed his bare chest. The entire time Morrie bathed her wounds, Louisa kept her eyes riveted on his face; his sandy curls, no longer contained by the full-head mask, framed his features. She studied the knit flesh of the mottled scar he bore from his hairline, past his ear, to the square of his jaw. She hardly noticed the sting and burn of her arms.

"This is my parents' home."

"And where are they?"

"Dead."

Bollocks. Of course, the sheets everywhere. "Why are we here? Why not downstairs?" Her voice sounded so far away.

"We need a place to work. To meet. My room in the pub is, perhaps, a little too cozy, and it's a lot less conspicuous up here—especially since you have a habit of showing up either bleeding or pissed off. My patrons don't need to know my personal affairs—or secrets for that matter."

Louisa flinched as he patted her arms dry.

"Can you stand?" he asked, kneeling before her.

She tried but nearly teetered over and sat down hard.

"Gotcha. Okay, I'm going to carry you over to the bed. Are you all right with that?"

She glanced at his bare chest from below

lowered lids and nodded. He swept her up into his arms. She laid her head against the smooth skin under his shoulder. He looked down at her, his lips brushing her forehead, or maybe that was her addled brain making things up. Morrie laid her down on the covered bed and placed her arms wound-side up. He brought over his medical bag and a chair with another length of damp cloth over the high back. Louisa watched him methodically string a curved needle.

"Isn't that for furniture fabric?" she asked, fighting sleep.

"Larger gauge ones are, yes, but this is standard field medicine equipment."

"Were you a surgeon?" Not a tactful thing to ask but her head wasn't working right.

"My parents put me through school to be a physician. They had no intention of me being a surgeon. But when I went abroad to find work in the Americas, what I stumbled into changed all that. Now, bite down on this." He placed a rounded piece of wood between her teeth. "Trust me."

Morrie tied a knot in his length of thread. Its cream coloration told her it was unbleached cotton.

Her brain locked onto the most mundane bits of information as the needle drew closer and closer to her skin. Morrie pinched either side of the gash, puckering it slightly. She shuddered and fell still.

It pierced her tender limb. She squeezed her eyes shut, bit down on the wood, and grasped handfuls of the drop sheet. But using her arm muscles hurt even more. Louisa spread her fingers wide instead, holding her body still as each new puncture sent a shock of pain through her.

She blacked out.

* * *

Thin gray light filtered between the crack in the curtains. Louisa sighed and rolled over. A sharp pain jolted her arm. She pushed herself up, the haze of sleep still muddling her senses. The room was too big and sparse and too —

"Morrie?" she whispered, confused. Then it all came crashing back. Louisa studied her wrapped arms. The leather under-corset of her mother's old lace gown dug into her ribs. She remained clothed exactly as she had been when he'd laid her on the bed.

Louisa drew to the edge of the mattress and stared at the man sleeping on the simple wooden chair. Drag marks in the dust led to the dressing table on the far side of the room. His mother's. Her gaze flickered back to Morrie, slouched in slacks and a shirt not fully buttoned to the collar, the sleeves rolled up haphazardly revealing his toned forearms. The full-body leather suit he wore to protect his identity was nowhere to be seen. *He probably went downstairs to change before coming to check on me.*

She flexed her hand. Bits of dried blood flaked like rust against the white sheet below. Her arms complained but no more than they might after a particularly brutal training session with Joe. Louisa smelled the bandage. *Frankincense and … lavender.*

On the bedside table rested a small jar labeled "Cut Salve." *The physician side of him.* She looked at her bandaged arms. *The surgeon side of him.* She looked at the man in the chair. *The reporter side.* Something in her longed to see the hero side again. She thought of his lips brushing her forehead when he held her in his arms, still uncertain if that was delirium or reality.

She stared at his torso. *He'd been bare chested.* Fire crept up her neck. She blinked the false memory away. Yes, he'd removed the upper portion of his disguise, but that was to allow for ease of movement when tending her wounds and to prevent bloodied water from dripping all over the leather.

He had not kissed her.

He was a perfect gentleman the entire time and had merely looked down to check on her before placing her on the bed.

Still, Louisa's heart fluttered as her gaze traced the thin, white scars crisscrossing up his forearms and under the rolled sleeves. They'd spider-webbed across his body, likely tracking around to his back as well.

I wasn't always a reporter. He'd told her that once. He admitted to studying to be a physician and ending up a surgeon. He knew field medicine and went to the Americas where something happened.

Louisa slid from the bed and leaned over to wake him, but the absolute peace radiating from his features stopped her. Something told her he didn't sleep well most nights. Besides, she knew the way out. Louisa grabbed the salve instead, tiptoed to the window, and peered through the crack. A tiny slice of orange split the bleak gray of pre-dawn.

No one would be up at Bennett's for at least another hour, maybe two, as he tended to sleep in on Sunday before heading out to church mid-morning. She hadn't gone to mass in over a year now. Not since before she'd placed her mother in the asylum. Living under his roof as Elenore's official chaperone meant both women would be joining him today.

Louisa slipped her arms back into the shredded sleeves but didn't bother to do up the buttons on the cuffs. She relieved herself in the commode and stared at her reflection in the vanity mirror.

Black smears covered her eyes in exactly the same spot her mask usually rested. *It's never left a mark before.* But during her fight with Scythe, when Louisa worked her way out of the headlock, her mask had flipped up. When she shoved it back down the polished leather side must have slid into place. The mask, having been part of an old pair of boots, still held layers of polish—which now raccooned her face, as Morrie had so graciously pointed out.

He'd said her secret was still safe. He knew Louisa better than Hersh did. The Inspector's snarl had come from being denied her identity. Between her sweat and the heat from Bug's flame launcher, one simple mistake with her mask had saved her reputation. She pulled at the polish on her face. It barely came off. *How in the Queen's name am I going to –*

Her elbow nudged a container on the back of the vanity. She was sure it hadn't been there last night. Louisa picked it up. A handwritten label stated "Shoe Polish Remover."

Of course. She smiled and tucked it into her coat pocket along with the salve. The leather driving jacket lay draped over the toilet seat. Louisa slid it on, wincing, and disappeared down the stairs. A twinge of guilt tugged at her chest. She couldn't just abandon Morrie after everything he'd done for her.

She looked around for stationary and finally discovered what the reporter had meant by working on an alternative place to meet.

The dining table sat linen-free holding files and

pages of news articles covering the rise of the Syndicate. A bulletin board clung to the wall above a credenza, holding all of Louisa's original sketches, strands of yarn connecting each one to various incidents and compiled information about the thieves. Even High Tower and Tater Face, the first two thieves she'd helped capture, were posted in the upper corner. A photo of the Judge from an old article covering his rise to Viscount rested in the center.

Louisa's heart soared. Morrie had gone above and beyond her expectations as a partner. This was absolutely perfect. After last night, she had a new sketch to add for their eyes only, and her brain already mapped the sharp features on a page in her mind.

She snagged a piece of paper from beside the typewriter and a pencil from a jar on the table. There was so much she wanted to write and not enough time to put it all down. It was better to say it in person.

Louisa snuck back upstairs and left the note on her pillow before disappearing from the house. She clung to the few shadows that remained an echo of the previous night and headed back to Bennett's house.

> *Dear Morrie,*
> *I cannot thank you enough for everything you've done.*
> *See you tonight,*
> *Phoenix*

* * *

THE LONDON CHRONICLE

From Thursday, October 19,
to Sunday, October 22, 1876

MUSEUM MAYHEM
By Morrison Tweed

Saturday night known thieves, Bug and Scythe, broke into the London Museum, knocking out four guards and setting fire to six of the interior wooden columns.

Though fire damage was kept to a minimum due to the fearless heroics of the fire department and their tireless workers, most of the canvas artwork suffered smoke, water, or heat damage.

Museum officials estimate millions of dollars in repairs and have closed the doors until the fire marshal has completed his assessment.

Insiders do not believe the museum will open for several months, if at all, unless a priceless ancient Roman artifact the thieves stole is recovered.

The water purification device found in the northern areological site at the Chedworth Roman Villa is purported to be advanced technology once used to filter gray water. Her Majesty, Queen Victoria, was said to be interested in researching how this ancient tech could improve upon current inventions.

Inspector Hersh claims that the city guardian, Shadow Phoenix, was caught leaving the scene of the crime, but escaped incarceration. She is wanted for questioning in connection to the fire and theft. He reiterates that she is not to be harbored or trusted, and is convinced she is in league with the thieves she previously identified and discredited.

However, none of the guards attacked are able to verify Hersh's claims. One guard does remember grabbing hold of Phoenix's ankle after she dragged him out of the fire to safety.

Arrest warrants are out for the aliases Bug, Scythe, and Shadow Phoenix.

THE METROPOLITAN POLICE

WANTED

BUG   SCYTHE   SHADOW PHOENIX

STILL AT LARGE

*L***500** BUG - Arson, B&E, Theft, Distruction. Midget.

*L***500** SCYTHE - Weapons, B&E, Theft. Filipino.

*L***1,000** SHADOW PHOENIX - Maiming, Vigilante Justice, potentially harmful technology. English.

DO NO APPROACH
EXTREMELY DANGEROUS
USEFUL TIPS WILL BE REWARDED

EPISODE VI
Masquerading as Yourself

Chapter I

Uninvited Guest

Louisa's mattress bounced. She groaned, her stomach jumping. With a cracked eyelid, Louisa Wicker assessed the perky young woman smiling eagerly—all teeth—nearly sitting on Louisa's lap. The brass base of the bureau clock glinted in the early morning light.

"Get off, Elly." Louisa rolled away, forcing Elenore Rathburn to the end of the bed where she took up temporary residence.

"Good morning, Lou," the young woman piped, altogether too cheerful for seven in the bloomin' morning.

After waking with her arms bandaged at the journalist's place at the break of dawn, Louisa had returned to the room she shared with Elenore at the home of her employer, Andrew Bennett. She'd only fallen back to sleep an hour ago.

"It's Sunday. Let me be."

"Oh, Lou, don't be such a spoil-sport. Andrew went into the workshop a few minutes ago. I'm sure he'll be expecting us."

Louisa opened her eyes wide and stared at Elenore. "Why on earth would he be expecting us? He gave me the day off."

The young pilot blushed.

"You said something to him, didn't you? Without asking me ..."

"Don't think of it like that. This is the perfect time for you to show me how to make the dispersal orbs. I can help you get back on track."

"Later, Elly. I'm tired. I made up a bunch last night."

"We have mass later and Andrew has scheduled a lunch meeting, and then we'll be out calling all afternoon. Come on, Lou. Show me?"

"Oh, all right. Get dressed. I'll meet you in the workshop in twenty minutes." Louisa pushed herself up on the bed with her palm. Pain lanced along her arm. She caught her breath.

Elenore leaned closer. "Are you okay? When

did you get to bed last night? You've dark circles 'round your eyes."

"Uh … fairly late." Louisa's heart squeezed. *Did I not get all the shoe polish off?* She rubbed her eyes and a faint smudge showed on her fingers. Her stomach jumped. Louisa rolled out of bed, away from Elenore. The young pilot clapped her hands, hopped off the bed, gathered her clothes, and disappeared behind the dressing screen.

Louisa scrutinized her eyes in the oval mirror above the dry sink. She poured fresh water from the pitcher into the porcelain basin and scrubbed her face raw. Elenore hummed as she dressed. Louisa gritted her teeth against the irritation. She wasn't in the mood to deal with a morning person right now. Not that she normally had any difficulty starting her day, but Louisa didn't do so because she liked to.

Elenore reappeared and pulled her nightgown down from the screen. Louisa patted her face dry. The two women locked gazes, and for a moment, Louisa was certain Elenore knew the truth.

"I've got just the thing, Lou." Elenore tucked her nightdress away and removed a jar of cream from her bureau, placing it on the end table between the two beds. "Three small daubs under each eye. Lightly blend into your skin. No one will be any the wiser about your late night." Elenore gave her a conspiratorial smile, winked, and slipped out the door. "See you soon."

Muffled steps whisked along the upper hall without pausing at the top of the stairs. Something told Louisa the younger Rathburn didn't miss breakfast for just anyone—Louisa included. She hung the towel beside the sink and caught her reflection again.

"Gah," she muttered and claimed the little jar.

* * *

Louisa straightened her vest and matching slacks as she hurried down the corridor. A good thing too. Bennett and Elenore jumped apart when Louisa entered the workshop. She narrowed her eyes at Bennett, fully understanding Reginald Rathburn's concern for his sister's reputation. It was one thing when Bennett forgot himself in the midst of a kind gesture, as he had so many times with her. But those had been innocent glances, smiles of encouragement, and brotherly affection—she saw that now. The high color on both their cheeks told Louisa a very different story.

"Good morning, Mr. Bennett." Louisa gave a cross between a bow and a curtsey. His gaze didn't linger on his assistant though. For that, Louisa was both relieved and concerned. She shrugged it off and gathered her leather work pouch from the pre-set table.

"Lou." Bennett gave a quick nod and busied himself at his desk.

Elenore hurried over. Luckily, she had the mind to wear one of her piloting skirts today. The flowing skirts could be buttoned together between the legs for greater ease of motion. Such skirts were usually used for cycling, but with the Inventors' Revolution, expectations for gender and class had blurred.

Louisa waved to an empty spot on the opposite side of the enormous dining-sized work table and Elenore scooted into place. She snuck a glance at Bennett.

Louisa cleared her throat. "Here are the materials for orb-making. It is important to layer the tiny glass filaments cross-wise around the small balloons." She demonstrated, blending each element as if she'd been making dispersal orbs her entire life. Louisa made sure to work steadily and pace herself. She glanced over at Elenore to see if she grasped the concept.

The young woman, not much older than Louisa, wasn't watching.

"As you can see" — her voice rose, startling her trainee — "it's important to strike a balance between china-thin walls and layered stability. If the orbs are too thick, they won't burst in the atmosphere. If they are too thin, they risk breaking before we can get them airborne."

The rosy hue in Elenore's cheeks expanded to her ears. This was a mistake. The pilot only wanted to spend time with Bennett. Louisa should've stayed in bed. She finished up the orb and set it aside to cure.

Elenore pulled forward a waxed cloth balloon. "Like this?" She mimicked Louisa's instructions almost perfectly. Maybe this would work out after all. Still, Louisa yawned. She'd rather be sleeping than playing chaperone.

An hour later, Elenore's crafting skills nearly

rivaled Louisa's, and they sprinted to see who could make more orbs than the other. They got so caught up in their game they didn't notice the hulking figure in the door until she cleared her throat.

"Good morning, Missus Courtright!" Elenore's cheery greeting startled both Louisa and Bennett.

The older matron, who ran the house for Bennett, stepped in and addressed her master.

"Sir, just a reminder that breakfast was ready twenty minutes ago, and the Landau will arrive promptly for ten o'clock to allow you time to travel to mass."

Bennett looked up from his disaster of a desk and smiled at the head housekeeper. "Ah, yes! Thank you, Missus Courtright. We'll be down presently."

She held up two identical envelopes. "These just arrived, sir. I shall place them at the table for you and Miss. Rathburn." She nodded to Elenore, whose expression brightened considerably. Louisa hadn't realized Elenore would take Courtright's reprimand so personally. The matron left with a piercing glare around the room.

Elenore finished up her orb and followed Louisa over to the dry sink. The ladies shared the basin water as they washed up. Louisa nudged Elenore with her elbow. A jolt of pain burst up Louisa's forearm. She held back a curse.

"Courtright's just like that. Even to Bennett sometimes. Don't take it to heart."

Elenore smiled and nodded.

"Ready, ladies?" Bennett called from the doorway.

They dried their hands and left for the dining room on the first floor. Louisa made sure to hang up her work pouch before following the goo-goo-eyed couple.

Downstairs, Elenore squealed as Louisa entered for breakfast. The young woman held a pale orange letter in one hand and a torn envelope in the other. Louisa sat beside her charge, across from Bennett. Warm, idle sunlight painted rainbows across the high polish of the dark table. Maria, the part-time servant who'd taken over Louisa's old duties, brought in cold meats, cheese, and a small pitcher of beer. Louisa held her stomach, trying to quiet it, as Bennett opened his matching envelope.

"Have you been invited, too?" Elenore asked him, simply giddy with excitement.

"Yes, it appears so. Should be quite the affair. I've never been to the viscount's estate before."

Louisa nearly inhaled her tea through her nose, and sputtered a cough. *Did he say viscount? The Judge?*

"A masquerade—oh, Lou! Can you imagine? We'll have so much fun."

Louisa raised her eyebrows and looked from one to the other, perplexed. Bennett cleared his throat.

"Elly"—he shifted his gaze over to Louisa who blushed—"you know what they say about assumptions?"

"Oh! Where are my manners? Lou, dear, Andrew and I have been invited to Viscount Fitzhugh's Allhallowtide masque."

"I do believe it has something to do with the growing celebrity of the cloud seeding project. Dear me, I should double check and make sure I've extended him an invitation to the presentation. Please excuse me." Bennett wiped his mouth on the cloth napkin and tossed it on the table by his plate before racing from the room and up the stairs.

Elenore looked to Louisa expectantly. "So, will you go with me?"

Louisa swallowed a groan.

Bollocks.

Chapter II

Bloodhound & Lame Duck

The moon flickered in intensity as thin, cirrostratus clouds flitted past. Still not enough condensation to prove worthy of bearing rain, but all that would change after Bennett's presentation at week's end.

Morrie's shapely, brown leather bodysuit twisted with his surprisingly fit physique as he looked down each side alley before turning right. The acrid stench of burned wood and smoke clung to the buildings surrounding the museum and nearby neighborhoods. Louisa held back a shudder—so much damage for no good reason. The Judge and his lackeys, Bug and Scythe, had to be stopped. It was up to Louisa and Morrie to retrieve the Roman artifact; heaven knew the constabulary were clueless. The Queen was highly interested in the ancient water purification process.

"Are you sure you're remembering correctly? It didn't take me this long to bust out of the paddy wagon at the museum," Louisa said.

Morrie waved at her to lower her voice. "They were running away. We're walking. You'd be surprised how quick Bug can be when properly motivated."

Louisa conceded. The halfling-thief had duped her before; she knew better than to second-guess him or his partner. The wraith-like cutpurse not only resembled a lethal weapon but also wielded several of varying sizes, to Louisa's dismay.

Morrie stopped. Louisa nearly plowed into him but caught herself. The triangle of fabric following the ridge of his nose cast shadows across his layered-glass eyes. That, and the patchwork nature of his leather bodysuit, emphasized his hawk-like stature.

"Why did we stop?" Louisa asked.

"Well, this is where I realized you weren't following and I back-tracked to find you."

"What! You said you knew where their hideout was. This is not knowing."

He stared at her from those hooded eyes, masking an expression she couldn't quite read.

"We're close. Bug said something before they parted about meeting Scythe at the main site on Pelham, just south of Kensington. I'm assuming he meant the Kensington train station. Pelham Crescent meets up with Fulham Road where a number of respected merchant shops are. Since the road curves around, I'll take this leg, you take the other, and we'll meet in the middle to report."

"Fine." Louisa gave a half-hearted wave, spun around, and dissolved into the shadows.

He should have followed them all the way back. We can't afford to let the Judge get away with manipulating the Crown.

Oh? And what do you think would have happened if he hadn't found you when he did? Louisa's cheeks heated at the thought and cursed her logical mind. She might have bled out, unaware that Scythe had hit her mark. They may have temporarily lost the artifact, but Louisa had lived to fight another day.

She shook off her thoughts and peered into the lower portions of upper windows and upper portions of lower windows, mostly catching glimpses of merchants tidying up their shops or sitting down for a late meal alone or with family. The respectable neighborhood did not lend itself to being a thieves' den. Then again, if the Judge's steward really was the go-between, he would blend in better in this area.

A pebble clattered over the cobblestones near the next establishment. Louisa shifted along near the wall, but not too close. These buildings had second and third floors with apartments and townhouses above the shops. She didn't need to go home smelling of refuse. Bathing too often would draw more probing questions from Elenore.

Stone-ground-on-stone with the hint of a slight slide-shift, nearly imperceptible. Louisa tensed. She crouched low and slipped around the corner of the building. Light spilled from an open cellar window. A denser shadow lurked beyond the pane. The opening stood large enough to slip through. Was someone waiting to enter?

All of Louisa's senses shot to high-alert.

Someone was there. The Steward? She bent deep into her stance, ready to spring an attack.

"Ugh! You're disgusting. For a midget, you

make a hell of a mess," Scythe spat, her voice wafting from the open window. The heavy shadow across from Louisa lowered. She reached for an orb and raised her arm.

A flash of brown leather caught in the faint light.

Louisa stopped before the release, curling the sphere back into her body on the downswing.

"Mor—Hawk?"

"What? Phoenix?" He shifted a touch more into the spill of light. "What did you call me?"

Louisa waved off his comment and re-pocketed the orb. She pointed to the window and held a finger to her lips.

"Am not. You're not doin' your share. I cook, you clean. We agreed—"

"You agreed. I ate," Scythe drawled.

"You won't eat again if that's your attitude."

"Bet they'll have quite a spread at the masque," Scythe said. "It's not right we don't get to go. No one would recognize us. Well, you might stick out, but I know how to dress for these things. Who is this contessa anyway? I've never heard of her. One of the Steward's specials, most likely."

"Duckworth said he saw her come in on a Spanish carrack. She's a widow of the house of Vega. Is living in exile for some reason."

"I don't like it. This is our gig. We shouldn't have to take second measure to some harlot just because she's got a foreign title. Call me Hari Tabak — *Sword God*. What's the difference?"

The slice-thud of a blade hitting wood carried out the window. Then another. Louisa pictured Scythe throwing her knives at a target on the wall, threatening Bug with each one she readied.

"It's here," Louisa whispered.

Morrie squinted at her and tilted his head to hear the thieves better.

Louisa shifted and readied herself to jump through the window.

"The difference is your face has been in the papers linked to highly public crimes. Hers hasn't. Even if that bootlicker Phoenix tries to claim the *Contessa* is a thief, no one will believe her. The police are after her too."

Morrie shook his head and held up a hand to signal *wait*.

Louisa scowled, both at his hesitancy and Bug's

comment. She still couldn't understand why Inspector Hersh thought she was a criminal. Sure, she'd made a mistake and hurt someone, but she'd never killed anyone and she'd never committed a crime. Louisa inclined her head toward the window again and shifted her stance.

Morrie grabbed her arm and pulled Louisa away. Behind the next building, he finally released her.

"What was that all about?" She whirled to face him. "We could have taken them by surprise, grabbed the artifact, and left them on the constabulary's doorstep."

"They don't have it, and if we left them for the police, they'd only be out again in a few months. Hersh would interrogate them, and they'd blame everything on you. Not the Judge or anyone else. They need to be caught in the act. Besides, now we know where their hideout is, we can keep closer tabs on them."

Louisa hated that he was right. They couldn't trust Hersh. "Dammit. And who says they don't have the artifact? They were just talking about needing to hand it off."

"The drop-point is the Judge's estate the night of the masque."

"Yeah, so?"

"So—"

A distant scream cut Morrie's comment short. The two guardians looked at one another, a sense of knowing passing between them. They took off running. A second cry cut short as they turned from Fulham Road to Sydney. A figure jumped onto the gabled roof in the well-to-do part of town. It slipped, landing on its derriere, and scrambled over to the wraparound porch awning and down to the ground.

Morrie pointed to Louisa and then up, and from himself to the ungainly figure hotfooting it down the street. They divided. She leaped from the railing onto the edge of the porch roof and climbed toward the broken window. A piece of dark gray fabric clung to a jagged shard. She avoided this and looked in. A woman in a nightdress sobbed as she covered the left side of the man's torso. He lay ashen on the rug, his nightcap askew.

"Are you all right?" Louisa asked.

The woman jolted, tears streaming down her

face. "Who are you?"

"Shadow Phoenix, ma'am. What happened?" Louisa carefully entered the bedroom through the window.

"We were robbed. Thornton tried to stop him, but he pulled a gun."

Louisa kneeled across from the woman. This was a case for Morrie, not her. "My partner is tracking down the thief. Where is your husband hit?"

"I don't know. I just covered up where the blood was."

"Lift your hands. Let me see." Though she wasn't certain she'd be able to do anything.

The woman lifted shaky hands covered in blood. The man gasped. Louisa ripped his nightshirt along the side of his body—nothing. She did the same for his arm. Relief washed through her.

"Just a graze. Let's tie up his arm to help staunch the blood."

"B-but there's so much …"

"I know. I know." Louisa grabbed the hem of his shirt, tore a length from around his legs, and wrapped it snuggly around the bicep. He groaned.

"Did you get a good look at the burglar?" Louisa asked.

"N-no. Young. He wore a mask and trim gray suit."

"Sounds like the man we saw running. Stay here. I'll alert the police. Keep pressure on his wound." Louisa carefully slipped back out the window and looked down the street. Two figures waned in and out of focus as they moved between the gas streetlights — one dragging the other.

Louisa hopped down, taking the same path the cutpurse had but keeping her balance the whole way. Morrie pulled the burglar into view. The young man held tightly to a velvet drawstring bag even as his head lolled.

"The cops are on their way." A whistle pierced the night confirming Morrie's statement. He removed a length of cording from his hip and tied the unconscious thief to the white picket fence.

Louisa looked up. The woman leaned out of the window and waved. Louisa waved back and held up the bag of jewelry before setting it in the thief's lap.

"Oh, thank you!" the woman cried.

Louisa and Morrie—Phoenix and Hawk—waved back and took off in the opposite direction of the whistle. A block away, they hid amongst the silent rail yard, its cars sleeping for the night.

"What happened?" Morrie asked, catching his breath, leaning against a freight car.

"Husband was shot. Nothing serious, just bloody. You should have been the one to go up there."

"You're a better climber. I'm a faster runner. Good thinking with the bag, showing her."

"No way would I let Hersh claim I stole the jewelry from the thief. It sickens me that we have to watch our backs even with the constabulary. We're on the same side! At least, I hope we are." Louisa wiped sticky blood from her hands onto her black hose. "We need to go back."

"Excuse me?"

"Not to the crime, to the thieves' hideout. We need to steal back the artifact."

"Think about it, Phoenix. Did it sound like they still had it?"

Louisa opened her mouth but the sharp reply

caught in her throat. He was right. She groaned and flopped her hands into the air. "Bug and Scythe have been forbidden to step foot on the Judge's property. The Contessa is now the carrier and will be welcomed at the ball because of her status with the nobility."

"Right. The way they were going on about it, they've already met her and handed off the item."

"Now what?" She sunk back against the railcar beside Morrie, deflated.

"We go to the ball. Did you get an invite?"

Louisa stiffened. Whether she said yes or no, her answer would give a little more of her identity away. She sighed. Morrie was right. The only way to stop the Contessa would be at the masque before she passed the artifact off to the Steward. And the best way to gain access to an event that prestigious and public was to be invited. She hadn't been, but she also knew Elenore would be happy now.

"I will be there," she said carefully. "And you?"

"I'll find a way."

"You'd better." Louisa stood tall and swept her arm out. "Will you be joining me tonight? It's still early."

"No." Morrie stepped toward her. "I want to do some digging into this Contessa and update the tracking wall back at HQ."

Louisa smiled at his off-hand reference to his parents' house above the salon. He hadn't been kidding when he'd mentioned working on a plan to keep her out of his room in the basement. Tonight, she'd hunt for trouble for a couple more hours before returning to Bennett's place. She walked away.

"Wait."

She turned back as he crossed his arms.

"What did you call me earlier? By the thieves' den?"

"Hawk. I can't be calling you by your real name when we're out in public dressed like this, right?"

"Why Hawk?"

"The nose." She pinched her fingers together above the bridge of her own masked nose, then gave him a wave and disappeared into the night.

Chapter III

Hiding in Plain Sight

"Oh, hurry, Lou! I don't want to be late," Elenore called from the other side of their bedroom door.

"Head downstairs without me. I just need another minute." Louisa stared at herself in the full-length mirror as the patter of Elenore's slippered steps marked her retreat down the hall.

Louisa stared critically at her reflection. She tugged her long, wild curls, which dripped with faux gray pearls. Louisa pulled away from the mirror, still uncertain. She descended the stairs in her high-heeled, black-patent fringed boots that accented the new matching leather bracers on her forearms. She had adapted a pair of archery armguards with metal plates and fitted them over her billowing black chemise like finger-less gauntlets. The under-bust corset cinched tight over her ribs and hips, while her mother's old lace gown tumbled in layers to a respectable length in the back. It threatened to reveal her knees in front had she not worn her tight black hose beneath. Louisa opted to trade her standard driving duster for a velveteen cape. It would better suit the evening's event. Still, it was a calculated risk to set foot in public as—

"Shadow Phoenix!" Elenore squealed, grabbed Louisa's hands, and spun her around in Bennett's foyer.

"Ready ladies?" Andrew Bennett popped his head through the front door and widened the opening to gawk at Louisa.

"Isn't she fabulous!" Elenore gushed in her Cinderella-at-the-ball dress complete with glass slippers. Delicate white lace embellished her light blue satin mask. The lady pilot glided over to Bennett, who stood tall, dressed in copper satin, wearing a bushy fox tail and dramatically pointed mask to match. Louisa caught him squinting at her. Her heart froze.

"Excellent use of that dress again, Lou. I almost

didn't recognize you."

Louisa let out a held breath. She'd worn it the night of the demonstration—the night she'd become Shadow Phoenix.

Louisa trailed behind but caught up with them as they exited onto the street, where Widow Abernathy's steam landau waited.

"Please, call me Phoenix tonight. And you shall be Lady Cinderella and Sir Foxworthy."

They laughed, all agreeing to keep their true identities secret until midnight.

"Oh, you all look so lovely, don't they children?" gushed Widow Abernathy. A wide-eyed boy and girl between the ages of seven and ten hid slightly behind their great aunt's voluminous skirts.

"Arthur will drive you to and from the estate tonight."

Her aged driver gave a salute from the front of the landau.

"I can't thank you enough, Mrs. Abernathy." Bennett kissed the back of her gloved hand. She waved him off.

"Oh, pish-posh, I'm honored." She turned to

Elenore. "You just be sure and tell me all about it tomorrow over tea."

"Most assuredly, ma'am."

As Bennett helped Elenore into the carriage portion, Louisa slipped a letter from her more stylish black pouch and passed it to the widow.

"Ma'am, if you happen to be looking for a governess, I'd like to recommend my mother. She will be back in town to stay by the end of the week and has—"

"Oh, my dear. I'm so sorry. The children's tutor travels with them. Their education is taken care of, but thank you for thinking of them." Abernathy tucked the reference letter and resume into her shawl pocket and, along with the children, waved to the group.

Louisa's stomach fell. She climbed into the coach unaided and sat beside Elenore, heart heavy. Her mother's final hearing and release were scheduled in five day's time, right before the cloud-seeding presentation to the Society of Engineers. She'd hoped to have stable, respectable employment for her mother by then. After tonight, she'd have no more down-time as they hurried to finish the last of the preparations for Bennett's big day.

"Buck up, Lou. This will be the party of the year," Elenore said.

Louisa tugged up a smile for her and Bennett and counted the seconds as the coach led her right to her enemy's door.

Elenore and Bennett dove into speculation about the grandeur of the ball and the rare fortune to be invited to the viscount's estate. Louisa filed away Elenore's head tilt, flirty eyelashes, and ready laugh, even as she mulled over the barely passable plan she and Morrie had agreed to. Everything hinged on the reporter getting himself invited to the spectacle of the season.

Masques, in general, were fun diversions well within the norm, but a masque on the weekend before All Hallows' Eve proved to be extraordinary. And now, with everyone in costume, it would be doubly hard to pick out the Contessa. If Morrie couldn't make it, Louisa wouldn't be able to do both her jobs at the same time. Chaperoning Elenore was just as important as recovering the ancient Roman artifact. When a woman's honor was at stake, almost nothing else mattered.

The landau chugged around the corner, off the street, and down a brightly lit drive to the viscount's estate. The friends fell silent and stared at the brilliance of the manor house and grounds. Traditional carriages vied for space next to buffed and shiny steam landaus parked along the left side of the drive all the way around the circular front and back up the parallel road out. Even a pair of ornithopters sat in the middle of the lawn.

Louisa's heart flip-flopped in her chest. She glanced into the shadows leading to the side grounds and the workroom in the old converted conservatory that belonged to Ryn, the princess-engineer. Louisa's hands twitched and her heart rate doubled. She jumped when Elenore linked arms with her.

The young pilot laughed and led the small group up to the receiving line, a half-step ahead of Bennett. Louisa didn't try to hold her back, though it was a tad improper. Two older couples and a matron with three daughters waited ahead of them. Beyond the wide double doors, Louisa caught the glint and guild of crystal and gold.

Her mother's voice invaded her mind. *Oh, Louanna, such balls and parties. You should have seen my debut. Layers of chiffon and silk petticoats with a different dress for every affair. When Mother and Father danced, my governess kept strict watch over me. Still, more than one beau found the opportunity to steal a kiss.*

Then her mother's cheeks would grow red as her past indiscretions dissolved the gay memories.

Never leave yourself vulnerable. Never trust a man, especially the married kind. When you return to that life, child, you will need to know manners, yes, but also remember to protect yourself. Your heart will lie. Don't listen to it.

"Oh, Lou, isn't it grand …" Elenore's voice trailed off.

Louisa snapped back to the present and the enormous ballroom.

"Phoenix," she whispered in her charge's ear as the opulence engulfed them. Louisa gasped at the fairy-quality of it all, not quite understanding all that her mother had lost until now. She knew she'd never rise to her mother's former standing and yet, somehow, the bastard child without a name had made it here tonight—all thanks to Bennett's belief in her.

"Here is your dance card," the manager said.

Louisa stuffed it into her pouch. She never would have made it as a dancer. Being unclaimed meant that her talent got her nowhere — as did refusing to spread her legs for the men of the Opera House. She was surprised they'd allowed her to stick around and clean the building as long as they had. So much for her mother's connections. Louanna Pierce simply did not exist.

Bennett guided the ladies through the crush of guests. Adorned in lavish costumes from prized silks to exotic one-of-a-kind dresses, the sons and daughters of prestige held masks on sticks up to their faces or donned full facades.

Strange. The room took on the likeness of a Dalmatian. Black spots, not men in tuxes, dotted the grandeur. One such mark passed Louisa and gave her a conspiratorial wink.

"Why, look, L — Phoenix! There are so many of you." Elenore giggled. It was true. Copycats took up her mantle as the disguise of the season.

"Better. Next time, drop the L, too, until after the reveal." That being said, she'd be the only Shadow Phoenix not in attendance at midnight. At least, not if she could help it.

The string section of the orchestra played a light tune not intended for dancing. Conversation hung heavy in the air. Bennett stopped to speak with several of his investors and their wives. Elenore was in good company, so Louisa signaled to her charge that she'd be back soon. She continued scanning the crowd, looking for Morrie or a woman of Spanish descent — though there was no guarantee the Contessa claimed the warm Mediterranean pallet. She really had no idea who —

"Phoenix?" A low female rasp stopped Louisa fast.

Louisa turned to the shadows by the hall leading to the refreshment room. Dressed head to toe in layers of pearl, the distinctive cut of her sari revealed what her tiger mask did not.

"Ryn! Thank goodness. I think we're the only sane people here," Louisa said with a wicked smile.

Princess Brynna Tamberlaine Fitzhugh, daughter of Viscount Fitzhugh and secret engineer extraordinaire, laughed and threw her arms around Louisa in an unexpected hug.

"It *is* you. I wondered if Father might

inadvertently invited you. You've altered your usual attire."

"Yes, well, my work boots, duster, and old half-apron might be more authentic, but that's not what tonight is about, is it?"

"Certainly not. The change is dramatic though. Striking. Were it not for your mass of curls and the cut of your dress, I might have missed you entirely. Love the pearls." Ryn reached out and traced a line of the soft gray balls alternating in size around a curl by Louisa's face. "Are they real?"

"Goodness, no. I—" Louisa gulped at the near slip. Ryn was sharp and any little clue might set her on the track to discovering Louisa's true identity. "I'm actually working tonight. Wouldn't want to risk losing real ones."

"Working?" Ryn glanced critically over Louisa's person. "But where's my gun?" Her voice hitched. Louisa had hurt her feelings.

"Now, Ryn, do you honestly think any of your father's attendants or retinue would allow me to casually walk into a major event such as this wearing a weapon, let alone a blunderbuss?"

The princess relaxed and nodded. "Yes, of

course. How is it going with your target practice?"

"I wish I could say I'm improving, but if that were the case, I don't think the museum would have gone up in flames last week."

"That was you?"

"No, that was Bug and Scythe. I'm here tonight to retrieve what they stole."

"Really? And how do you intend to do that with all these people about and my father's men on guard?"

"Umm … very carefully?"

Ryn let out a hearty laugh. "Well, then, tonight I might just stick around to watch the fun. Did you come alone?"

Another loaded question.

"I'm with a small group, and I'm hoping to meet my partner —" *Codswallop*, pertinent information.

"Your boss you were doting on?"

Louisa smiled. "No. He's here tonight, but I've resolved that issue. We're friends. Well, more like long lost siblings. It just took me a while to figure it out."

"Does your partner know who you are?"

"No. We share the same goals though, and that's enough."

Ryn raised her eyebrows. Louisa just laughed. Then the princess's merriment transformed into a scowl. Louisa followed her gaze up to the small stage on the far side of the room.

"If you'll excuse me, I'm being summoned." Her voice oozed contempt.

Louisa couldn't blame her. The Judge kept her locked away most of the time only to call on her to do his bidding and create the unique weapons he needed for his thief-minions.

The Judge, better known as Viscount Fitzhugh, raised a speaking-trumpet to his lips, at the front of the stage. The orchestra and guests fell silent.

"Welcome, welcome, ladies and gentlemen. It is my great pleasure…"

Louisa tuned him out and joined the gentle wave of moving bodies, riding amongst them like a cuttlefish. As the Judge blathered on, Louisa scouted the crowd. She recognized the voices and builds of several of Bennett's investors, as well as those earls and dukes who oft found themselves mentioned in the gossip rags.

The Judge presented Ryn, his faithful daughter, to the crowd. The scowl on her face tugged her mask into a strange configuration. Louisa had to smile even though her stomach twisted. Ryn was not one to be crossed lightly.

Morrie had been less than forthcoming about how he planned to crash this party and had said even less about how to identify him once he was there.

The orchestra struck up a lively polka, and Louisa found herself in the middle of a sea of partners. She caught sight of Bennett and Elenore. Louisa nodded at them as they danced by. Unfortunately, her momentary lack of peripheral perception caused her to jostle a couple behind her. *I have to get off the floor!* Louisa turned and apologized, looking up into a pair of dark eyes she'd never forget.

Chapter IV

What Time is it, Mr. Wolf?

L ouisa glared at her father. Clayton Richard Emsworth's thin lips and angular jaw framed the lower half of his mask. The very nobleman who'd sullied his governess and tossed Marie Pierce out into the cold, pregnant and dishonored. A scorching fire ignited within Louisa's chest, threatening to burst free of her lips.

He broke eye contact with her and danced away with his wife. Somehow, still staring at the couple, Louisa managed to back herself out of the sweeping crowd and into a portico — one of several niched along the west side of the ballroom. A heavy presence loomed behind her. She'd left herself vulnerable. One of the Judge's men had picked her out of the crowd and —

"Is your dance card free?" The deep baritone

soothed her electrified nerves. Louisa turned to face a man in steel-blue tails ornately filigreed with silver, wearing a full, feathered blue-gray hawk's mask. He held his arm out to her. Louisa smiled up at him and a lightness filled her body, making her almost giddy.

Morrie.

"Apparently, gray hawks are more fashionable than brown, or so my tailor tells me."

She accepted his arm as he led her back out onto the dance floor and swept them in amongst the other merry-makers.

"Are you all right? You looked flustered."

Louisa glanced over her shoulder, disgust, betrayal, and longing mixed with a volley of other emotions all vyed for dominance, but Morrie's hand across her upper back cleared her head of everything but his nearness.

"I'm fine. No, really. I just ran into someone I haven't seen in a long time."

"I must say, I didn't figure you'd be so on-the-nose with your attire." He lightly fingered the beads in her hair. "I like the softer touches. A tad impractical for your usual evening attire, but quite lovely, considering the venue."

Louisa blushed and hit his shoulder. "You're one to talk. So, I'm assuming you haven't spotted her yet?"

"The Contessa remains elusive" — he turned left and Louisa hopped in time to the music — "but she wouldn't have come alone. Wouldn't be proper. She would likely have arrived on the arm of someone invited. Someone in the know but not well-known. We need to narrow down as many attendees as possible to see who we don't know, and who we do, who might have escorted her. And search for the lady herself."

"What do you mean *narrow down*? Everyone is masked. I'd be lucky to identify a handful of people here even without their masks."

Morrie chuckled. "There's a trick to it. First, we eliminate older couples. Look for gray streaks and cotton tops, or men's hands that have age spots — it's not foolproof, but you'll start catching the clues. The Contessa is a younger window and would not be seen with an older man."

Louisa scanned the dancers closest to them and found, to her surprise, that several couples fell into that category.

"Next, we strike the green debutants. They'll

be, on average, the most up-to-date and flamboyant with their fashion. And you can strike any of the men they're dancing with. Whoever the Contessa came in with will not want to draw attention to himself, nor will he be ungentlemanly and take a spot on a younger *chit's* dance card."

He looked her up and down, a cocky smile playing over the half of his mouth not covered by the hawk's mask. "I'm impressed, Phoenix. As distracted as I'm trying to make you, you remain incredibly poised and sure-footed, light even. Your body flows seamlessly with the music, and you adjust with the slightest of touches. Joe mentioned you were a dancer, but I had no idea."

Louisa fought yet another blush. "Once upon a time I tried to make it in the business, but circumstances prevented me from being taken seriously." She shrugged.

By the end of the dance, they had narrowed their search from a crammed ballroom of strangers down to twelve potential targets — six women and six men. Louisa was tasked with finding a way to discretely get asked to dance by the gentlemen and then to subtly grill them for information. Morrie had to find his way onto each lady's dance card before the exchange happened. They had to establish who the Contessa's contact was before it was too late.

Louisa checked in with Elenore and slid between Bennett and her charge before the young woman had a second dance with him.

Bennett startled. "Oh, L—Phoenix. Did you enjoy the first dance?"

"Yes, thank you. I need to speak with Lady Cinderella for a moment. I think I heard Mr. Green's voice just over there. He's the environmental engineering gardener, right?"

Bennett laughed and shook his head, looking around for the botanical expert. Louisa waved toward the nearest gilded sconce to show him and then led Elenore in the opposite direction.

"But—" Elenore glanced over her shoulder at Bennett before giving Louisa her full, wide-eyed attention.

"May I ask how many balls you've attended since your debut?"

"What? Oh, maybe three or four in half as many years. Traveling with Reggie makes it difficult.

"And did your brother instruct you regarding etiquette?"

Elenore frowned. "He said to be polite, not talk of the weather 'cause it bored men and didn't show off my mind, and he said never to dance too close even when waltzing."

"That's it?"

"Yes, why?"

"There's so much more your mother would have taught you. I take it you and Reginald have been on your own for some time?"

"Yes."

"All right then, here's the fast version of what you need to know. If someone asks you to dance and your card is not full, unless you are feeling decidedly unwell, you accept. No matter what. You do not, however, dance with the same man more than once unless you wish to cause a stir or announce your intentions either for courting or engagement. If you insist on dancing with Bennett again, allow him to take the last dance. This could either be read as him showing an interest in you or him being polite since you are a business guest staying in his home. Do not kiss him—"

"Lou!"

"Don't give me that. I see the way you two look at each other. I will be watching, but from a distance. I have my own business dealings I need to attend to. I won't hover around you, nattering as a proper chaperone should, because I trust you. Don't give me reason not to. Understood?" Louisa couldn't help but bite back a bemused smile. Here she was, seventeen and the daughter of a society outcast, giving advice to a pedigreed nineteen-year-old.

Elenore nodded as a gentleman approached. He bowed to the young pilot, complimented her on her recent win at the Battersea Races, and asked her to dance.

Louisa nodded.

Elenore accepted.

Louisa refocused on her mission and weaseled herself into a conversation about the coming cloud-seeding presentation with a group of men consisting of two of her marks for the evening. By the next dance, one had offered her his arm. The problem was, not only was he not connected with the Contessa, but after two more strategic dances, word had traveled about her skill on the dance floor — that and her eccentric topics of conversation. Suddenly, she had multiple offers to dance and no way of getting acquainted with her last three marks. At one point, over half-way through the evening, she digressed to talking about the weather and purposefully stepped on a partner's toes.

She apologized and begged off the remainder of the dance due to dizziness. Louisa caught a mirthful glance from Morrie, who danced with yet another of his marks. A flash of pearl caught Louisa's eye, and Ryn swept by with a dashing red-haired (certainly not a popular color but great for annoying her father) Scottish fellow whose brogue was so thick Louisa wasn't certain if he complimented the princess or spoke about his farm. Ryn had her sly smile painted on, and she looked just over her suitor's shoulder, tracking something with her gaze.

Louisa followed Ryn's stare all the way back to her red-faced father. Ryn had admitted to Louisa once that she didn't linger at these events. But earlier the princess had hinted that she might stick around a touch longer with Louisa present. Louisa hadn't expected to see her friend dancing. Still, anything to get under her father's skin.

At the end of the set, Ryn almost mechanically disengaged herself from her partner. She headed straight for Louisa, linked their arms together, and steered her down the hall to the refreshment room.

"Now that was fun." Ryn passed a glass of Champagne to Louisa. "I can't dance to save my life, but the expression on my father's face was more than worth it. Seamus is a duke, too, so it's not like he can complain. How goes the mission?" Her eyes twinkled over the tip of her glass as she took a sip.

"Terribly. I can't get to my other three marks for men wanting to dance with me. Gah. And now I fear they won't want to risk it because of the latest diversion. I'm going to miss my chance, Ryn. The Contessa will make the exchange with your father's man, and I—"

Louisa caught a flicker of movement down the hall, a blur of red followed by a trim blue-gray. *Morrie.* She grabbed Ryn's arm and pulled her down the hall, stopping at a door half-way back.

"Where does this lead?"

"The servants' area, lower kitchen, and cellar. Why?"

"Can you keep an eye on Elenore Rathburn, the pilot, for me? She is Cinderella in powder blue tonight."

Ryn made a face, a cross between contempt and disgust.

"I'll owe you one."

The princess's expression brightened.

"Thank you!" Louisa squeezed her friend's hands and burst through the door, flying down the steps. At the bottom she looked left. The sharp tip of a blade pierced Louisa's cloak above her leather corset and pressed into her flesh.

"Well, well, well … the real Shadow Phoenix."

Chapter V

Will You Do the Fandango?

"My employer will be most pleased when I bring him a dead bird." The woman's round phrasing and sultry lilt sounded more Italian than Spanish to Louisa, but that thought disappeared fast. The blade penetrated her skin.

Louisa dove forward, pulling a lightning sphere from her pouch. She tumbled and sprang with a twist, smashing the orb at the Contessa's feet.

The viper jumped back, pulling a hand-fan from within the folds of her gown. The orb's blast refracted off the metal stays of its razor-sharp tips. Louisa's gaze fell on a gray-clad leg angled on the floor out a doorway. *Morrie.*

The deadly edge of the fan whipped toward her neck. Louisa arched, deflecting the weapon with her new arm shield. Twirling opposite the blow, Louisa shot her leg out and knocked her attacker back. The Contessa faltered, tripping on her crimson skirts. Louisa dove, aiming her shoulder to the woman's stomach. A satisfying *oof* accompanied the solid connection.

A knee crashed into Louisa's side. She gasped, rolling off the viper. Another volley of slices sang through the air. Louisa ducked and rolled before standing and deflecting two more strikes of the lethal fan. They parried and dodged, lashing out at one another in a frenzied dance. No matter how many times Louisa got past the Contessa's defenses, the woman retaliated with poise and grace.

Louisa shoved the villain into the wall, drawing curious stares from the kitchen down the hall. The Contessa staggered back, winded, and pulled a tiny silver derringer from between her breasts.

Two burly attendants tromped around the far corner, sending the furtive on-lookers scattering. Louisa pulled another sphere from a separate area of her pouch and smashed it to the floor, ducking low. Thick smoke filled the corridor—a new lightning blend. A bullet lodged in the wall where Louisa's head had been. She fled, every step driving another spike of fear into her chest.

Is Morrie all right? Did she shoot him? If he's hurt – But she couldn't think of that now.

Louisa slipped into a storage room and held the door shut behind her. The small, dark space amplified each shaky breath. *I should have brought my gun.* No. It wouldn't have mattered. The bullets served only one purpose. Perhaps she'd have to rectify that.

When her heart settled enough that she could hear again, silence greeted her. Louisa cracked the door open and scanned as far along either side of the corridor as possible. She opened the protective slab of wood farther and risked poking her entire head through the gap.

No one.

Blast. That meant the men were only a diversion and the exchange might already be happening. *Bootlicking muntz-watcher!* Louisa cautiously retraced her steps back to the corridor by the stairs.

Empty ... except for —

"Morrie," she whispered, dropping to her knees beside his prone form.

He groaned. She helped him sit up. Morrie held his head and rocked forward. Louisa caught his shoulders and kept him from tumbling into her.

"Morrie, are you okay? What happened?"

"She caught me off guard and hit me over the head with something metal." He shook off the memory and held Louisa's arms tight. "She told the Steward where she hid the artifact. It's by a statue in the middle of the grounds. You have to go, quick!" He tried to push her up.

"What about you? I — "

"I'm not important. Go!"

Louisa scrambled backward, looking over her shoulder as she climbed the stairs into the brightly lit corridor above. Her heart screamed at her to return to Morrie even as her brain listened to him and compelled her forward. She had to find a way out.

Bursting through the upper kitchen, Louisa startled the wait staff. She dodged exclamations, curses, hands, and serving trays — some purposely aimed at her head. She crashed out the back door onto a patio lit with soft gas lamps. As Louisa hopped over a marble railing, a darkened glass building caught her eye, reorienting her as she dashed along a cobbled walkway lined with box-shrubs.

A tall, thin shadow moved in the distance. Even in the dim light of the garden she knew that silhouette — the Steward. Ignoring decorum, Louisa jumped over the hedges delineating the well-manicured labyrinth, landing each stride on the balls of her feet as she might with a *jeté* leap.

Joe, her trainer, had only ever given her one, pure compliment, perhaps more of an observation, but Louisa never forgot it: *Yer not made fer flat-footed brawlen'. Yer a dancer, so dance. The rhythm is yours. Own it an' you'll be unstoppable.*

Louisa was far from being "unstoppable," but she'd learned to trust her instincts. She vaulted over a taller hedge and sank to her knees on the other side, hidden by a three-foot weigela readying for winter.

The Steward stood, hands on hips, surveying the area not twenty paces away. Louisa watched him through barren branches, not daring to move. He studied the statue of the goddess Athena, slowly pacing its perimeter. Three times he disappeared around the far side and only returned twice.

"*Bollocks,*" Louisa whispered. She shifted as far right as the hedge maze would allow but still couldn't see the man. The far left was no better. Another dead end. If she tried to jump over one end or the other, she wouldn't make the extra wide distance. She had to go directly for the middle or risk backtracking and wasting precious time.

Again, Joe's voice invaded her thoughts. *Use what God gave ya an' stop thinkin' with yer eyes.* Somehow, over the past three weeks training with Joe, his voice had replaced her mother's as the voice of reason—at least in times like these.

Louisa settled low into her crouch, rocking her body and closing her eyes. A hint of cologne lingered on the breeze, but nothing definite or trackable. A soft grinding, *perhaps stone on stone,* carried to her from the other side of the statue.

Then nothing.

No footsteps, no heavy breathing, no abnormal

rustling—just night. Louisa's heart climbed higher up her throat the longer she waited.

Dammit. He was gone. Down a passage under the statue or across a lush stretch of lawn. Didn't matter. She'd missed him.

Louisa opened her eyes and leaped over the hedge. She ran to the far side of the statue and—

—right into a horizontal staff.

The hard wood cracked against her lower ribs.

"Ugh," she groaned, doubling over the stick. It swept away. Louisa looked left into a mauve wall. She twisted away as the Steward's walking stick collided with her shoulder.

He's still here! Louisa's heart beat her from the inside as the Judge's man throttled her from the outside. She whipped her arm out to grab the staff, but he yanked it back and swung at her shins. Louisa jumped, stumbling sideways, arms out for balance.

"The Contessa warned me you were here, Phoenix. This ends now."

Louisa snatched an orb from her pouch, deflecting another blow with the opposite arm. The staff hit skin and bone instead of her reinforced armband. Her shot went wild and hit the statue several feet away from her mark, sending a sizzle of electrified dust into the air. The Steward swung at her again. She rotated her forearms to block each calculated strike. He moved like a fencer and yet somehow different.

If it wasn't knives, fire, or guns, it was something else entirely. What was it with these people?

Blow after blow she struck only connected a handful of times. Louisa made each hit count. Pain spidered across his features, but it hurt her as much as it did him. *It's not enough.* A glint of metal caught her eye. Something nestled between the marble folds of Athena's gown.

The Steward swung for her head. She ducked, punched him in the kidneys, and swept his feet out from under him. Louisa dove for the artifact, gathered it to herself, and rolled through a controlled tumble. The heft of the object strained her bruised body, but she grasped a Ryn-made lightning orb and slammed it down behind her. The added boost helped propel her forward. She leaped over the nearest hedge, arcing back around toward the mansion.

Certain she heard cursing and branches breaking, Louisa ran for her life, keeping the taller grasses and sparse trees between her and her pursuer. The stone and metal Roman artifact dragged at her, reminding Louisa of every hit she took that night and during her run-in with Scythe at the museum a week ago.

The grand house loomed large. She stumbled into its deep shadows, not seeing the Steward but fearing the worst. She couldn't bring the artifact into the masque; she had to hide it. Desperate, Louisa clung to the shadows, fighting to control her breathing, determined not to gasp in pain. Inch by terrifying inch she made her way toward the conservatory, wishing tonight hadn't been the one night it was left dark. Still, that didn't mean Louisa couldn't get in —

After stashing the object in the one place she knew no one would look, Louisa opted not to travel through the house back to the ballroom in case the Judge had more goons on patrol. And the last thing she wanted was a run-in with the Contessa. Louisa had no way to defend herself from a gun. But she couldn't *chasse* through the front doors either since the night grew long and no one would dare arrive that late to the party. Besides, she didn't have an invitation to present.

Louisa held her arms around her sore ribs as she deked around the estate, holding court with the shadows and keeping a keen eye out for the Steward; for anyone. She ran up the sweeping stone steps onto the closest balcony, following the strains of a fresh waltz into the over-bright ballroom crammed with people and color.

She scanned the walls, searching for a familiar face.

A hand clamped on her arm, yanking her around mid-stride.

Chapter VI

Do as I Say, Not as I Do

Louisa's stomach jumped. She gasped for air and every muscle in her body tensed as she prepared to run. But the grip changed. A gray mask appeared, and a familiar hand settled in the small of her back.

"There you are." Morrie's deep rumble melted her fear. He swept her effortlessly in amongst the dancers, hiding her in plain sight amidst the myriad of other Phoenixes.

"Did you find—"

Louisa hugged him, fast and firm, cutting off his words. She pulled back when her logical self caught up with her emotional self. Heat flashed up her neck to her cheeks.

"I'm sorry."

Morrie placed a quick finger on her lips before

reclaiming her hand and moving Louisa into a turn. They danced far closer than she ever had with anyone else. But no one paid them any mind. No one but Ryn anyway. Louisa watched the princess's eyebrows raise before she pointedly went back to monitoring Elenore and Bennett as they danced.

Last dance already?

"There's no need to apologize." He said something else, but between the hum of the crowd, the orchestra so near, and the large clock above the bandstand drawing her attention, she didn't hear him. The second hand twirled around, coaxing the minute hand ever closer to midnight.

"Phoenix?" Morrie asked, the sound of her name returning her to the moment.

"Pardon?"

"I said, what happened? Did you find the artifact in time?"

"No. Yes? Sort of. The Steward knew I was coming and waited for me. Beat me soundly with that staff of his." She shuddered, feeling every welt and bruise acutely. "But I got it from him and hid it where no one will ever think to look for it."

Morrie guided her between the brightly lit

couples: fairy creatures, sea maids, princesses, and animals. His long legs glided between hers, mimicking each step as if they'd been doing this their entire lives.

She glanced at the clock again as he twirled her out onto the smaller, middle balcony — the one without steps leading to the garden below.

"Is that possible? You never left the estate, did you?" His words caressed her ear; soft, warm, distracting...

"What's that now? Oh, no. It's safe. I shall retrieve it later. It'll make for a long night, but there's nothing to worry about."

The song ended. A cheer rose from the ballroom. Louisa glanced over her shoulder and watched hundreds of masks fly into the air. Laughter and excited talk claimed the orchestra's space. Morrie bowed, removing his mask. Louisa curtsied and winced.

"Are you certain you're all right?" He set his mask on the ledge and ran his hands up her arms to her shoulders. The thin chemise did almost nothing to separate his skin from hers. Louisa's heart quickened.

She gasped but didn't pull away. "Just bruises. They'll heal."

The moonlight illuminated a red welt on Morrie's forehead, above his right ear. Louisa gently shifted a sandy lock aside, allowing her fingertips to caress the wound.

"It's nothing. The Contessa caught me by surprise." He leaned into her touch, eyes half-closed.

Louisa raised her other hand and trailed soft touches along the mottled scar running from the opposite temple down to his lower ear. Her gaze lingered on Morrie's lips and something inside broke free. She closed what slight gap remained between them and kissed him. His warm mouth parted, welcoming her. Heat radiated between them. Morrie's hand swept from her shoulders down to her back beneath the cape, toward the small of her back. He pulled her in. She ached for him.

What are you doing! Her mother's voice shot ice through Louisa's overheated body. She stiffened and pulled away, her heart reaching for him even as she caught his confused gaze.

"I'm sorry," she spoke low, *sotto voce.*

A flicker of knowing crossed his face.

She turned and leaped from the balcony.

"Louisa, wait!"

But she dared not look back. Dared not go back, even as butterflies warred with rainbow lightning in her stomach. Instead, she ran. Ran as far from the reality of her emotions as her feet could carry her.

At the front of the estate, a steady flood of merry people surged down the steps and along the drive. Louisa caught sight of Elenore and Bennett, arm in arm. She waved and hurried over, stepping between them and linking arms with Elenore.

The young pilot dressed as Cinderella laughed. "Oh, Lou, between you and the viscount's daughter, my modesty and reputation are quite intact. Reggie would be pleased."

Louisa forced a smile and a chuckle, her insides still at war. Bennett led the ladies back to Mrs. Abernathy's landau and held the door open for them. The women gathered their skirts and collapsed on the bench opposite Bennett.

Elenore chatted happily the entire drive home, into the house, and up the stairs. Excitement clashed with exhaustion as she enlisted Louisa's help with the stays on her ballgown before donning her nightdress. She tumbled into bed. Her soft snores pattered the air, helping Louisa stay awake, waiting for her chance to re-dress and collect the artifact from the credenza in Ryn's workshop.

The moment Elenore shifted and her snore quieted, Louisa's stolen moment with Morrie flooded her synapses. She groaned, curling in on herself, wanting to remember the taste of his lips and the heat of his hands, but knowing she'd crossed a line.

Louisa threw off her covers. The chill air attacked her body and cleared her mind. Morrie's final cry echoed in her head. She froze mid-step. He hadn't called her Phoenix... He'd called her —

Louisa.

Chapter VII

Listen to Your Mother

Louisa stared at the orb supplies laid out before her without seeing them. She kept feeling Morrie's warm hand cup her back as he led her effortlessly through the waltz. Louisa marveled at how light his footwork was. His grace and poise matched her own. She couldn't claim to have a similar upbringing, but there were parallels. His merchant-class father did his darndest to make sure Morrie would fit into polite society just as Louisa's mother had with her.

She closed her eyes and once again his lips parted, accepting her kiss...

"Right, Lou?" Elenore asked, breaking Louisa's trance.

"Umm, pardon?" Louisa blushed and looked

back and forth from Elenore, who worked beside her, to Bennett, who sat in front of stacks of paper at his desk.

Elenore laughed. "Case in point."

Louisa gave Bennett a quizzical look.

"Elly was asking about the dapper stranger who whisked you off your feet. Did you discover his identity at the reveal?"

Should I say? What have I to hide? And yet…

Elenore nudged Louisa with her elbow and smiled.

"Oh, that was nothing. Just Mr. Tweed feeling sorry for me." Overly warm, Louisa stood up. Had either of them seen her hug him and would they call her out on it? "If you'll excuse me, I need some air. I'll be back in a bit." Before either colleague could respond, Louisa strode from the room, smoothing the creases from her slacks.

Courtright stood at the bottom of the stairs, giving Marion instructions for how to properly clean the electrical chandelier in the sitting room. The young woman eyed the A-frame ladder leaning against the banister.

Louisa met Courtright's gaze and held it as the

housekeeper spoke to the other woman. She inclined her chin toward the workshop and raised her eyebrows. Courtright gave a curt nod and an approving half-smile as Louisa grabbed her coat and headed out the front door.

Courtright had been borderline civil with Louisa since learning Bennett fancied Elenore and not his assistant. Even though the matron agreed with the match, she also clearly sided with Rathburn, Elenore's brother, about needing to keep an eye on them to prevent scandal. Especially now, when Bennett was so close to earning the Queen's approval and making a name for himself.

Louisa stepped out into the brisk, late October morning. The breeze cooled her cheeks and cleared her mind. Mrs. Abernathy stood at the foot of her steps, directing her driver/houseman where to hang the cross on her door and exactly how to place the jack-o'-lantern on the stoop.

"A little more to the left. Yes, that's it, Arthur, you've got it now." The older widow caught sight of Louisa and waved her over.

"Good morning, Mrs. Abernathy. Lovely day. Getting ready for tomorrow night?"

"A good morrow to you, too, Miss. Wicker. Yes. I do like to be prepared. The soul cakes are cooling and the children have chosen their disguises."

"And how are they settling in?"

"They are used to traveling with their parents and find staying in one place a pleasant treat. That and I'm probably spoiling them too much." She gave a throaty chuckle. "You know, I've been thinking about your mother arriving soon and wondered if the two of you would like to come to tea. I know you'll be busy with Mr. Bennett's big presentation this weekend, but perhaps before the hub-bub your mum might like a moment to re-connect in a quieter atmosphere."

"That is very kind of you. She would be delighted. I'm picking her up this Friday in London. She'd like to stop by a few preferred shops before settling in, but I'll be showing her around in the afternoon." She'd be doing nothing of the sort but gave a general wave toward Bennett's place.

"Perfect. I'll expect you ladies for tea at three o'clock then?"

"I can't wait." Louisa inclined her head and made to leave, but Abernathy touched Louisa's arm.

"Oh, just a moment, dear. I'll be right back." She bustled off into the house and returned with a jar of crabapple jelly.

Louisa smiled.

"I know I just passed along some the other day, but word has it the young Elenore Rathburn is partial to it too. They do make a lovely couple."

"Indeed." Louisa accepted the jar and slid it into her coat pocket. She'd pass it along to Bennett after her walk. "I'll be sure to get it in past Isabel." Louisa winked and carried on her way, feeling anything but jovial and light.

She had no idea where she headed, except that she needed the exercise and the air. Yes, her mother would be "home" in three days. Louisa still had no apartment and no job for her. Frankly, Louisa didn't know what to do.

She stifled a yawn. Between last night's late adventures and waking up early to work on orbs for the cloud seeding presentation, she'd barely slept. Still, the artifact was back in the right hands. And Morrie... she couldn't think of the dashing reporter with the mysterious past without a mix of longing and confusion.

She'd slipped up. All night her dreams replayed the echo of him calling her real name. She had no doubt he'd kept a mental catalog of clues about her identity ever since they'd met, but last night when she whispered to him... those two words in that tone gave her away. As Louisa, she'd schooled herself to speak low and light in his presence—the opposite of Phoenix and how she spoke with those who knew her.

Not once did Louisa think the reverse—not to speak low when she was Phoenix. And now the reporter who'd named her Shadow Phoenix, who'd followed her exploits and even partnered with her to stop the Judge, knew her real name. Or at least the name she went by. That meant he also knew who had taken liberties and kissed him.

Her stomach flip-flopped and her pulse quickened. She tried to shake it off, taking deep breaths. Morrie wouldn't expose her true identity. They were partners. But if she felt like this when he wasn't even around...

She finally understood what her mother must have endured when Louisa's father seduced her. And Morrie wasn't even trying. She'd made the first move.

"And it will be the last." But as much as Louisa's head agreed, the rest of her body rebelled.

She stopped before a steep set of familiar stairs. Louisa's feet had brought her home. She climbed the steps, knocked on the door, and entered the boarding house she'd moved into the same day she'd abandoned her mother in the asylum. Freshly baked bread and sweetmeats engulfed Louisa's senses. Her knees weakened and she leaned back against the door for support.

Miss. Margaret Applewood hurried out of the kitchen and down the long hall to the foyer, wiping her hands on her apron. A smile spread across her round face at the sight of Louisa but faltered the closer she got to the young woman. The kind, plump landlady did not stop several feet away to greet her boarder, as decorum dictated. No, she swept Louisa up into a robust hug.

Louisa leaned into the protective embrace her own mother never bothered with. Regret stabbed at her insides, but Marie Pierce had never been one to withhold the truth, including that the world was cold and mean. Miss. Margaret led Louisa to a chair at the kitchen table and put the kettle on. She patted

Louisa's clasped hands and returned to kneading the dough for meat pies. The round metal baking dishes sat lined along the counter by the sink.

"Now, what's troubling you? Come on, you need to get something off your chest. Out with it or it'll curdle your insides."

Louisa gripped her hands tighter, staring at them. Miss. Margaret could always read Louisa.

"It's, it's ... my mother. She's coming home this week and I —" This wasn't what Louisa had meant to say, but she went with it. "I need to find her a place to stay. Would it be all right if she took over my room until I return? That should give me enough time to find somewhere for her."

"Of course she can stay, love. And I'll even hold Mr. Cliff's room for her as he'll be heading to the Americas at the beginning of the month. Going to make his fortune, he is. Your mother can take up residence on the top floor, if it suits her. You say she's a governess? 'Twould be a wonderful space for tutoring."

"Yes, I agree, but we haven't secured work for her yet. Maybe just a room for now? Is the one down the hall from mine available? I know you like to keep at least one open for travelers, but…"

"That's fine. I can put the travelers in the suite until someone more long-term comes along. But I'm sensing this isn't what's really bothering you. It does have to do with your mother though?"

Margaret Applewood folded the dough with her fists while looking at Louisa with her keen blue eyes.

Louisa sighed. "In a roundabout way, yes. I, I really don't know how to say this." Her insides twisted. *Ladies don't speak of such things in polite company*, her mother chastised.

"Just out with it, dear. I've heard it all. Nothing surprises me."

Louisa blushed, then got mad at herself. She'd been doing nothing but blushing since last night. She gripped her hands so tight her fingers threatened to break. At least the physical pain distracted her from the internal ache.

"Go wash and then help me with these."

Louisa slipped out the back door and used the pump to splash cool water over her hands, careful not to be wasteful. With the drought, Miss. Margaret's well ran dry regularly, and she had a whole house of guests to run.

Back inside, Louisa dried her hands and then coated them in flour. She helped her landlady transfer the flat, doughy circles over to the pie tins. They worked together amiably.

A timer dinged and Miss. Margaret removed the bread from the large pot-bellied wood stove. She passed Louisa a pot of blended meat, potatoes, and carrots. Louisa filled the pies while Margaret set the tops on. As they worked together sealing the edges with practiced pinches, everything bubbled out of Louisa.

"I think, no, I know I'm sweet on — I mean, I like someone. I need to be careful. In fact, my mother always told me to keep my distance if I ever suspected …Well, I can't. See, we work together. No, it's not Mr. Bennett but someone helping him who I've been dealing with on his behalf. We both attended the viscount's masque last night and, well…"

"You got on pretty well? Danced?"

"Yes. And …"

"He kissed you?"

"I kissed him. I couldn't help myself. I don't

know what came over me. He was being a perfect gentleman, doing and saying all the right things, looking so kind and handsome—" Louisa gasped at her revelation.

Miss. Margaret chuckled.

"I can't follow my mother's advice. I need to work with him." *And so does Shadow Phoenix.* "I'm not going to pursue this, and I know he won't either if I ask him not to, but … Oh, Margaret, I'm not even around him and he affects me. What will I do when I actually see him? My mother always said not compromise myself, but what if I'm swept away again? What if it goes farther than a kiss? I'm all in a tizzy. I can't concentrate on anything, and Bennett needs me at the top of my game. I've quite lost my senses. I'm confused, but I'm also afraid. Afraid …"

"Afraid you'll end up like your mother?"

Louisa's eyes widened. She bit her lip and nodded. "How did you know? I've never …"

"You said it all just now. Yes, mothers are very careful about these things, but the way you've repeated certain phrases, and the absolute terror plastered over your face, says more than you know.

You've also never spoken about your father. It doesn't take a genius to piece it all together. And this is why you've come to me instead of her? You fear her wrath?"

"Yes. But I also know she won't tell me how to, um, to protect myself. I'm not a harlot. I'm, I'm…"

"Trying to be practical?"

"I just want to shield myself, and that is knowledge she will never share with me."

Margaret set the pies in the oven, wound her timer, turned back, and grasped Louisa by the shoulders. "Then I will teach you."

* * *

THE LONDON CHRONICLE

From Thursday, October 26,
to Sunday, October 29, 1876

A ROYAL NOD
By Morrison Tweed

In a surprising turn of events, Her Majesty Queen Victoria has issued the following statement:

"Though circumstances surrounding the theft of the museum's artifact one week ago were highly suspect, we cannot deny that the city's professed guardian has sent a clear message with its return."

In the wee hours of the morning on Monday, October 30, a concerned citizen witnessed a figure cloaked in black strike lightning in Buckingham Square. Guards on duty recovered the stolen Roman artifact along with a note signed by Shadow Phoenix.

London's purported masked guardian clarified the events surrounding the horrific fire at the museum and singled out the known thieves, Bug and Scythe, as being at fault.

The constabulary refuses to comment except to say that it is Phoenix's word against the Inspector's. Inspector Hersh states that he caught Shadow Phoenix exiting the burning building, but also admits to arriving after the heist had taken place.

Her Majesty's personal secretary relays the Crown's appreciation for the recovery of the discovery of the century.

EPISODE VII
Missteps & Misdemeanors

Chapter I

Driven to Distraction

"You can finish this in the morning, you know." Louisa crossed her arms and stared Bennett down across his explosion of a desk.

He shifted a stack of papers to reveal a file, but not the one he searched for. "I know they're here. I'll find them and then call it a night. I promise."

A knock traveled up from the front door.

"I'd better relieve Elly. She has a big day tomorrow. She's been all nerves thinking about it," Louisa said.

"She'll do fine." Bennett kept saying that, but this was the young pilot's first multi-ship command, and her brother wasn't around to help her. Louisa headed for the corridor.

"You will be there, right?" Bennett asked as if reading her thoughts, though still clearly distracted.

"Yes. We're on track. In fact, we're making extra dispersal orbs now in case any of the casks are damaged on the way over to the Sky Port."

"Excellent, excellent …"

Louisa hurried out onto the landing.

"Make sure she has some of Isabel's special chamomile tea," he called absently.

"I will. Now find those RSVPs and get off to bed." Louisa rushed along the open upper hall to the stairs just as Elenore closed the front door and placed the tray of soul cakes on a small round table usually reserved for traveling gloves. A sad smiled played across her lips before she met Louisa's inquisitive gaze.

"Oh, it's nothing, I suppose. No, that's not true. I just find it hard this time of night. The children's disguises are always so fun to see, but after ten o'clock it's the poor folk who come." She glanced over her shoulder out the window set in the door "Bonfire's nearly out."

"Yes, I'll monitor things now. There shouldn't be too many more."

"I'll stay with you." The hint of uncertainty in Elenore's tone gave away her concern over leaving before her duty was done.

"You'll do nothing of the sort. You are to ask Isabel for one of her special teas and then go to bed."

But the young woman didn't glance down the corridor to the kitchen; Elenore looked up toward the workroom instead.

"Don't worry about Bennett. He'll be retiring soon too. Go on now."

Elenore nodded and shuffled along to the kitchen. Two more desperate souls knocked at the door. As it neared eleven o'clock, and no one tended the dying fire at the end of the street, these would likely be the last two wanderers of the night. She gave the bedraggled women the last four soul cakes.

"And who shall we pray for, Miss.?" The petite one asked.

Louisa did not know her extended family and thought it odd to send prayers to them. She'd never been on this side of the All Hallows giving before.

"Pray for the honorable Mr. and Mrs. Johnathan Rathburn." Louisa had heard Elenore mention her parents' names a few times that evening.

"Certainly, Miss." The taller woman curtsied, collected the spiced cakes, and both women dissolved into the night.

Louisa refreshed the candle in the hollowed-out gourd sitting on the step. A light shuffling whisked by behind her. As Louisa locked the door, she kept one eye on Elenore. The young pilot paused outside the workroom but didn't linger. Louisa watched her walk all the way down the corridor to their shared room, before heading to the kitchen herself.

She listened at the door and made sure Isabel wasn't still hard at work preparing items for baking the next day. It was nice that she and her husband got to stay in the basement — late nights were just a flight of stairs away from home.

Louisa nibbled on a soul cake left out on a lunch plate as she waited for the house to fall asleep. Unfortunately, her mind buzzed. The Judge had ordered his minions, Bug and Scythe, to make sure Bennett's presentation to the Society of Engineers bungled. She had to brainstorm with Morrie, her new partner in crime, about how to stop them in broad daylight. But the last thing she wanted to do was see him again after what had happened at the masquerade.

Finally, Bennett settled for the night, and Louisa snuck back into the workshop to slip into her own disguise.

* * *

Louisa kept to the shadows as she made the thirty-minute walk across the Thames River to north London near Bishop's Gate and the Spitalfields. Joe had given her the week off training since she wouldn't know what evenings she might get away or for how long.

Bug and Scythe, the Judge's henchmen, weren't going away, and their boss would demand an encore to their failed attempts at sabotaging Bennett's cloud seeding presentation. Morrie had agreed to monitor Bennett's warehouse, but they still had to plan for the unexpected on the big day.

And yet, Louisa did not end up at headquarters. She found herself standing in the shadows on the grounds of the enemy's estate, watching the old conservatory door. Her gaze flickered occasionally to the thin patches of light that escaped from around the painted panes.

She stood at the door a moment, listening to the room beyond before she knocked.

"Come in," came Ryn's distracted tone.

Princess Brynna Tamberlain Fitzhugh stood regally in a gold silk sari embroidered with purple. She had her hands on her hips, eyeing her matching headscarf, woven into a strange netting, which lay on the worktable of her shop.

Louisa hesitated just inside the door. The hairs on the back of her neck rose.

Ryn looked at Louisa decked out head to toe in her usual black Shadow Phoenix attire, the embellishments of two nights ago stored away. Louisa raised an eyebrow as if asking how to proceed.

Ryn cracked a sly grin and belly-laughed.

Louisa shut the door and joined her.

"You know"—Ryn smoothed down her flowing sleeves—"I was just thinking, *if Phoenix were here, she'd have the biggest I-told-you-so waiting to launch from her lips.* And not a moment later, you come waltzing through my door. Poetic justice, I suppose."

"If you're calling me a devil, you might be

right. Anything's possible on Halloween." Louisa flashed Ryn a wicked smile right back.

"So, now the question is, have I ruined it or will the electricity still conduct with the natural fibers woven in?" Ryn mused.

"Electricity, you say? What on God's green earth are you designing now?" Louisa stepped up to the table, her woes about Morrie and Bennett all but forgotten.

"Lucky you came by. My father has gotten some ridiculous notion in his head about the electrical current being the next big revival. If you ask me, it's bulky, cumbersome, and damn finicky stuff to work with. Edison was right to abandon it. Still, my father has his eye on a modification Bell is tinkering with in the Americas. Knowing my father, this has more to do with stopping someone else's progress than forwarding his own. Did you know that Joseph Hansom is looking at revealing a new landau at the Frost Fair?"

"Is that so? Is your father backing Hansom?"

Ryn frowned and pressed her lips together. "I'm not sure. I doubt it. Either way, I think it's linked somehow. I overheard him dictating a letter yesterday, hinting that he'd gotten insider-information about the new design, and then he found me and got me started on this new weapon."

Louisa stared at the finely woven net on the table. "This is a weapon, not a tool?"

Ryn's gaze flickered from Louisa's face to her hip, where she absently pushed the long duster aside to scratch an itch.

A smile burst across the engineer's face. "You're wearing it."

Louisa looked down and lifted the modified blunderbuss from the holster she'd made and held the flame-disrupting weapon in both hands reverently.

"Always, when I'm not attending my mortal enemies' galas that is."

Ryn laughed and held her hands out for the long, flare-barreled gun she'd nicknamed *Phoenix* instead of the usual *Dragon*.

"How is she behaving?" Ryn asked like a proud mother.

"Exactly as you designed her to. My aim is improving, but practice is difficult right now. Still, better than even two days ago. However, besides your lovely company, I came to see if you could help me create a new type of ammunition." Ryn still had extra wax from Louisa's last request for practice blanks, though Louisa had no idea why Ryn was helping her—except that the engineer liked a challenge and had befriended the vigilante, maybe out of spite to her father. "See, lately, I find myself getting shot at."

"And you'd like to shoot back?"

"Precisely. But—"

Ryn held up both hands, palms out. "No. Don't tell me. You want a gun that shoots people but doesn't actually kill them."

"Um, now that you say it out loud, it does sound rather ridiculous."

"Yes and no. When you fire a proper handgun, your *poor aim* might inadvertently cause you to kill someone. This weapon is lethal only at short range—and only if you hit your mark. Hmm …" Ryn turned the weapon over in a slow, gentle manner.

"Really, I'm looking for something that works similarly to my lightning spheres—gives off a kick, will knock someone over on impact, not maim or kill them in the process. But I can't get the ratio right with the smaller spheres the gun uses. I thought maybe you might know of something else I could use—other than black powder."

"Perhaps. Can you swing by tomorrow? I need to finish this project for my father, and then I have a few ideas I could try. We can do target practice to see what works best."

Louisa swallowed. Last time, Ryn had shot an anti-fire round into her woodstove, and the resulting blast could have alerted the constabulary, not to mention the household.

Ryn handed the blunderbuss back to Louisa and returned to work, re-absorbing herself in half a heartbeat.

Louisa didn't bother saying goodbye. Ryn's invitation to return said it all. But as Louisa folded herself within the shadows along the edges of the estate, she knew she couldn't return home just yet; otherwise, she'd be worse off than Elenore—tossing and turning all night. She had to clear the air with Morrie. She owed it to Bennett to remain focused. She owed it to herself.

Chapter II
Patent Pending

Louisa took a run at the brick wall at the back of the alley and scaled it with relative ease. She dropped into the postage-sized yard and straightened her duster as she stared at yet another door.

Her gaze fell to the upside-down cracked flowerpot — the decoy — and settled on the gap in the ground between the flagstone and a mass of weeds still thriving in the fall chill. A dim light oozed beneath the bottom of the door. Louisa nabbed the spare key. She squared her shoulders and opened the door, her heart creeping into her throat.

Morrie stood dressed in his form-fitting, patched-leather Hawk suit; the myriad of brown hues highlighted the contours of his body. He leaned over the old dining table, sorting through papers. Louisa's gaze lingered longer than it should, but the crisp snap of each discarded sheet drew her focus.

She cleared her throat — or tried to. Little sound came from its dry interior. Louisa glanced away and stared at the photography equipment stashed in the corner of the room. Morrie straightened regardless and turned toward her, a file in one hand and a page in the other. His lips lifted from scowl to smile.

"Loui—"

She held up her hand, and curled her toes within the confines of her boots, trying to ground herself. Her teeth found the fleshy bit of inner cheek as Miss. Margaret, her landlady and surrogate mother, had taught her. Louisa clamped down briefly on the tender flesh to tame her surging emotions.

"Phoenix, please. Yes, you know who I am now. We're on the same footing. I hope you're not disappointed." She extracted a shaky breath and held up her hand again to stop his retort. "I think it's important we remain professional. You should continue to call me Phoenix, and I'll call you Hawk. During the day, when we're unmasked, we will refer to each other as polite society dictates — using our surnames."

"I don't understand." Morrie set the documents down on the table and stepped toward Louisa, his stance relaxed and far too at ease for maintaining professionalism.

Louisa tried to breathe through her rising panic. If he got too close, her determination would wane.

Look at a point to one side of his face. Don't make eye contact until the sensation has passed, came Miss. Margaret's voice. Louisa did as instructed.

"I made a mistake and over-stepped at the masquerade. I am entirely to blame, and I apologize for being so forward. It won't happen again." The words tore at her guts, but she couldn't allow what had happened to continue. It wasn't proper.

"Won't … won't happen again?" Morrie crossed his arms, still perplexed.

"That's right. We're business partners and our … *relationship* should reflect that. Don't you agree?"

He tilted his head slightly and regarded her with cool gray eyes before turning away from her, back to the table. Louisa recoiled as if punched.

"I've spent the last two days digging up what I can about the Contessa. I have a feeling we haven't seen the last of her." Morrie's tone held a confrontational note.

The cold shot hit Louisa a second time. Perhaps he had only been polite in kissing her back, hadn't— She shook the thought from her head and walked 'round to the opposite side of the table.

The more space you can keep between you, the better, Miss. Margaret reminded.

"Do you suppose the Judge might use her at Bennett's presentation to the Society of Engineers?" Louisa asked.

"Perhaps. My money is on Bug and Scythe, though, based on what we overheard a few nights ago at their hideout." He echoed her thoughts but grew quiet again. The stiffness in his back and shoulders worked to unravel Louisa's determination. Morrie had never acted like this before.

"I think we might have another problem," she said.

Morrie quirked his head to the side again. He

gave her nothing tonight.

"Ryn's working on a new gadget. Says she overheard her father talking to the Steward."

"What's the hit?"

"I'm not sure. Maybe the patent office. The Judge is convinced a new way to use electricity, or something similar, might be what is behind the coming innovations of the Hansom Cab Company's newest landau. The model is set to exhibit at the Frost Fair."

"What? That makes no sense. Why would he steal a patent that's already in use?"

"Don't ask me. Ryn seemed to believe that if the patent disappeared, no one else would be able to apply the theory either. Which would explain a lot if the Judge has shares in Hansom's company."

That gave him pause.

"I think he's being paranoid. I mean, we all know the limits of electric power. It's a novelty at best," she said.

Morrie nodded. It was his fallback response most of the time, but tonight it felt different — distant.

"Still, I suppose if the princess is working on

something new to support this, we should at least look into it. When is it supposed to happen?" he asked.

"I don't know. Not tonight. She's still working on the project. Maybe tomorrow, Thursday, Friday? I doubt they'll do anything the day of the presentation, and they won't want to let it drag on either."

"Yes, that makes sense" — he dropped the file to the table and leaned forward on his hands — "but it doesn't. I don't know. I would've heard if there was a resurgence in working with electrical energy from my sources."

"So, what, then? Do we just ignore it?" If he wouldn't back her up on this, she'd do it alone.

"No, but we'll need to be careful. I'll see if I can find the patent they're looking for. Maybe if I read the theory, it'll make more sense." He grew thoughtful, staring out over the table rife with notes, and up at the bulletin board of thieves. "And we'll need to contact Hersh."

"What's that now?" Louisa stiffened.

Morrie's scowl deepened. Louisa wasn't sure if it was because of her or something else.

"The Judge still has an order out to destroy Bennett's cloud seeding presentation, whether it's Bug, Scythe, the Contessa, or someone else entirely who does the deed. Phoenix and Hawk won't be there to save the day. That means we'll have to convince the constabulary to do it for us."

"I know that, but Hersh? We still haven't confirmed if he's working for the Judge. He hates me. Why would he help me? There must be someone else we can reach out to."

"I don't think so, on both accounts. Hersh is just a blighter. I'll look into him. If we can convince him Bennett's project is still a target, the extra police presence could be enough of a deterrent. Regardless, if the Judge's minions do try something, the constabulary will have to be the ones to deal with them. You know we can't just leave them gift-wrapped like that burglar the other night."

"Hersh will never trust me. He thinks I'm one of them. But if you want to waste your time working that angle, be my guest."

"You're being unreasonable, Phoenix."

"Am I? A certain reporter very clearly stated

how the constabulary, and Hersh in particular, feel about the whole Shadow Phoenix situation. I'm a wanted suspect. I— Just forget it." Louisa pulled a sheet of paper from her leather pouch and slammed it on the table. The Contessa glared up at them from the sketch.

Morrie turned his back to her, waving her off.

Louisa left the way she came. It was late. He was brooding, and she had to play chaperone in the morning. As she hopped back over the garden wall, Louisa couldn't shake the emptiness hollowing her out. This wasn't how she wanted to leave things between her and Morrie. But what had she expected? For him to ignore her request and pull her into his arms? No. That only happened in dime novels.

Chapter III
Of Mice & Women

Bennett held the passenger door of Widow Abernathy's steam landau for Elenore. He offered her his hand to help her out and then almost forgot to extend the same courtesy to Louisa. He gave his assistant a sheepish grin before walking with them across the open field to the south-west Sky Port's lower station house. The dry, brittle grasses crunched beneath their feet as a buzz of activity drew their gazes skyward to the elevated moving sidewalks.

A giddy Bennett nearly skipped ahead, chatting about the quality of the morning, as Elenore dropped back, shuffling her feet. Louisa glanced from the five moored mini-airships above to the woman falling behind.

"You go on ahead, Bennett. Elly and I will

follow." Louisa slowed and fell into step with the young pilot.

Elenore looked down, hunched her shoulders, and closed her body. Louisa wasn't going to be trite and ask what was wrong. Instead, she halved their pace again and linked arms with Elenore.

The young woman took a shaky breath and tried to laugh it off, but it came out more like a sob. "Oh, Lou. What shall I do? There are five of them."

Louisa squeezed her friend's arm. She knew Elenore didn't refer to the Minis floating above. The two women watched Bennett disappear into the long, low building attached to the Sky Lift.

"You know what they'll be thinking ..." Elenore's voice trailed off.

"I do. But you've got this."

"No. I don't. I thought I did, but the closer and closer today got, the less assured and prepared I felt. Lou, my mind is absolutely blank. I'm a fraud. Winning the Battersea Races was a fluke. I didn't do it alone ..." Her breathing quickened.

"I know. I was there." Louisa winked.

Elenore gave a wavery chuckle, then gulped.

"Why did Bennett choose you?" Louisa asked.

"Because Reggie wasn't available."

Now it was Louisa's turn to laugh. "True! But after him, why not one of those five men on your team? Why you?"

"Because I won the race. Well, *we* did. He needed a celebrity to help bring attention to the project." Elenore's tone dropped again.

"Yes, indeed. And, other than being a woman, what makes you so special? Have those men ever won the Races?" Louisa nodded to the group of pilots exiting the station with Bennett.

"No."

"Have they ever flown with the famed Reginald Rathburn formerly of Her Majesty's Royal Air Force and one of the most decorated pilots in all England?"

"No," her voice came stronger.

"Does that make you better than them?" Louisa tilted her head to look right at Elenore.

"Noooo …" She shook her head at the same time.

"Does that make you qualified to lead this team?"

"No!" Elenore looked at her with surprise.

"Then what does?"

Elenore opened her mouth to retort, a fire burning behind her eyes.

"Hold that thought. Now, when you address them, speak as you would be spoken to and show them what Reggie, Bennett, and I know about you. And remember, *you* won that race. I just managed not to mess up."

"And here she is, gentlemen, Miss. Rathburn." Bennett gave Elenore a slight bow and waved her forward. Louisa unhooked their arms and stood a half-step behind her charge; close enough to lend the support of her presence, yet far enough to show her respect for this remarkable woman.

Elenore gave a tentative smile to the semi-circle of male pilots, all around her brother's age or a bit older. Louisa watched the young woman's furtive gaze flit from face to face before staring skyward.

"They certainly are beautiful, gentlemen."

The men followed her line of sight, startled by Elenore's comment.

"I'm particularly drawn to the azure blue one. Have you noticed the sleek curve of her cab's hull and the slight angle to the side flaps? Remarkable.

Now, take a look at the emerald Sky Runner. I've always admired the hollow ribbing used —" By drawing the men's eyes away from Elenore to assessing one another's Minis instead, the young pilot was able to stand taller and speak as a professional — without a stutter. She was the very model of grace and dignity and awareness. Elenore didn't only touch on the positives of each ship either. She singled out the one major flaw each model sported and asked probing questions about how the men handled the challenges.

" — in fact, I'd love to see how you've overcome the drag that particular design has struggled with. To have come this far, your modifications must be truly unique," she praised.

Bennett waved at someone over Louisa's shoulder as the five pilots eagerly amassed around Elenore, and the group made their way toward the Sky station. They talked almost as one entity, now eager for Elenore's official inspection of her crew and their ships.

"Lou, can you handle this? I know you're not partial to the skywalk or the lifts," Bennett asked, then turned to follow the others without waiting for a response.

A presence filled the space behind Louisa. She turned to see who Bennett had waved to. Her heart quickened at the nearness of loose sandy curls and bright gray eyes.

"Mor — Mr. Tweed. What are you doing here?"

Morrie smiled a far more wicked grin than the question warranted.

Louisa blushed. No trace of last night's anger blemished any part of his aspect.

"My job, Miss. Wicker. Having five up-and-coming male pilots being led by the first woman to race and win is quite a story."

Louisa frowned and faced the reporter head-on. "Don't you dare go asking questions and interrupt Miss. Rathburn's first meeting with her team. She's nervous enough without having to deal with you too."

Morrie held up his hands, laughing. Laughing! He stepped into Louisa's personal bubble of space and leaned toward her conspiratorially. "I wouldn't dream of it."

Louisa's tongue stuck to the roof of a mouth gone dry. Every nerve ending in her body alight, she nearly passed out. *What is he doing?* It was a complete one-eighty from last night.

"I'm here to observe, not intrude." He swept past her and sauntered over to the lower station.

Louisa's heart and stomach flipped spots before the one jammed into her throat and the other dropped to her knees. She looked heavenward, but not to speak to God—to gather strength from the multitude of milling bodies on the skywalk above in order to join them. Morrie might not intend to interfere, but his very presence could affect Elenore's focus. Louisa had to act as a buffer. The Lord knew she couldn't entrust that job to Bennett. He was as giddy as they come and didn't fully realize the impact of this moment on anyone but himself.

Louisa caught up to Morrie as he entered the lift. The open-air cage had the capacity to hold six people comfortably, but as the doorman operated the counter-weights to raise her and Morrie up, Louisa's heart plummeted to join her stomach. She wavered in the small space and clung to the wrought iron bars as it ascended beyond the station roof.

Morrie shifted closer, somehow blocking her

view front and side. The porter mostly blocked her other side, and the stiff iron at her back tricked her into believing she wasn't dangling hundreds of feet in the air from a single core of cables. Louisa breathed in Morrison Tweed's light, woodsy cologne and closed her eyes, imagining them anywhere but trapped in midair. The image that corrupted her time and again was that stolen kiss on the balcony at the masque. Heat radiated from his body. She almost leaned into him.

"Skywalk, port side," the porter announced as the hinges to the barred door creaked. Louisa opened her eyes to Morrie's trim Norfolk jacket. She glanced up, startled by the conflicted look shadowing his features. He turned away and held an arm out to indicate she disembark first.

With a slight wobble, Louisa mounted the platform. The false sense of security this area offered was almost enough to keep her stationary. But Elenore stood with Bennett and the pilots on the next berth over—and that meant willingly stepping onto the mechanical walkway. It was, by sight, far more robust than the temporary platforms strung above Battersea Park for the races, but it was still an open-weave netting between the walkway and the shoulder-height brass rail. Louisa's knuckles went white as she gripped the platform rail. Last time, she'd braved this insanity for Bennett; this time Elenore needed her.

As Louisa pushed off the railing and stepped toward oblivion, Morrie's familiar arm hooked through hers, and he escorted her to the walkway. Again, her body threatened to betray her. She wanted to cling to him, to feel his solid mass against hers—but no.

She bit her lip and counted backward from 100 in her head, as Margaret had instructed. At the next platform, Louisa whispered a thank you, as proper manners dictated, and slipped away from the man who just last night agreed to keep things professional between them. She didn't know what to think. One moment he was cold and abrupt, the next warm and helpful. But she detected something else in the way he moved today and in his general proximity to her person.

Luckily, Elenore's words distracted Louisa back to the task at hand. Morrie stayed true to his promise and stood far enough away so as not to be a nuisance. Actually, it was Bennett Louisa had to keep an eye on. He kept trying to put his own two pence into the conversation, each time throwing poor Elenore off her train of thought. The man didn't realize he was as much a distraction to Elenore as Morrie was to Louisa.

So, Louisa abandoned the reporter, who was now behaving himself, and she linked arms with Bennett, tugging him slowly away from the flock of pilots. She did not let go, even after the men began asking questions of Elenore about the project and their role in it. Bennett continued to migrate toward Elenore without even realizing it. Louisa kept nudging him back toward Mr. Tweed, who missed nothing. In fact, Morrie caught Louisa's gaze for a moment and his eyes shone — a mixture of mischief and merriment. Yes, Louisa caught the irony of the situation. She permitted herself a grin.

"Morrison, we're heading to brunch with the Greens at a quaint little tea shop in London. Would you care to join us? Might provide an ideal time to chat with Miss. Rathbun about this morning's inspection."

"Why, thank you, Andrew. I would be

delighted, as long as I'm not intruding?"

"Not at all, my good man. Nathan and his lovely wife enjoy a good party, and after this morning's stress, we all need to let off a little steam."

The two men laughed.

"I think I'll head back to the office, Mr. Bennett. I hope you will make excuses for me?" Louisa asked as Elenore wrapped up the morning by taking a tour of the mini-airships. Each cabin was so small, it didn't take long.

"What? And miss our pious gathering for All Saints' Day?" He grinned at Morrie and rubbed his stomach.

Louisa purposefully avoided eye contact with the reporter. "I'm afraid so. You still haven't found that batch of RSVPs, and we need final numbers for the Sky Port's caterer. I'd also like to finish that spare barrel of orbs so we're not rushing right before the presentation." Really, only half of that was true and he knew it.

Bennett's gaze clouded. Had she overstepped? Had she over-embellished and now he warred with himself about going back early and joining her?

"Sir, your job right now is to ensure this is the presentation of the year. You can't do that stuck behind a desk. You need to be *seen*. This is why you have an assistant. I will keep everything on track behind the scenes while you do what needs to be done out here."

He knew Louisa was right, but she saw that familiar expression that told her he also knew she was avoiding being in public for some reason. How had they become so familiar with one another in such a few short months?

Elenore shook hands with each of her team members and returned to the smaller group, beaming with pride. She locked gazes with Louisa and gave her a big smile; one Louisa willingly returned.

* * *

The hansom cab Louisa hired dropped her off in front of Bennett's townhouse. She paid the driver and walked in through the front door, catching herself mentally replaying the first time she'd ever dared use the privileged entrance — the night of the demonstration. When had walking in the front door become so commonplace? When had the trepidation and undeserving attitude been replaced by normalcy?

Louisa couldn't answer that.

She was glad, though, to not be part of the luncheon. She'd initially looked forward to the affair, but Miss. Margaret had warned her to limit her time around Morrie in order not to risk losing her head — or her heart. As it was, she still couldn't get over his actions at the Sky Port — almost beyond gentlemanly.

And yet, why would he be … what? Flirting with her?

He'd never done so before.

Had he wanted to?

But they'd agreed to keep their relationship professional.

Did he know he was doing it?

She had to believe he did.

Louisa had known she'd intended to kiss him, even if she shouldn't have — was compelled to. But she'd made every effort not to repeat her folly.

She climbed the stairs to the workshop, feeling a steady gaze follow her. Louisa wasn't entirely sure where Courtright stood, but the housekeeper was always aware of everything that went on. Louisa gave a general wave before entering the workshop. She halted just over the threshold and sighed.

Bennett's desk was a war zone. Louisa welcomed the distraction. She used the extra space on the workbench to organize files, papers that needed filing, notes, letters, pens, pencils, inkpots, and so on. She found the misplaced RSVPs between two documents near the bottom of the pile on the left side of the desk.

Once she'd removed and collated everything, Louisa assessed the state of the desk overall and how best to help keep Bennett organized once he returned. She pulled open the narrow central drawer just over the knee space and then the deeper drawers to either side. Louisa removed the few papers and pen nibs left scattered behind before grabbing a few calling cards stuck to the bottom of the drawer.

She froze.

The card on top wasn't from a casual caller or interested backer—it was Inspector Hersh's. Morrie's words echoed through her head. *They'd only be released in a month or so … they'll say you worked with them … Hersh needs to catch them in the act.*

He was right. She hadn't wanted to admit it. Louisa wasn't like Bug and Scythe and the Contessa; she valued life and refused to take it from anyone. If those cutpurses were going away, she'd need a man at the top willing to do it—even if it meant taking her out too.

Chapter IV

Three Blind Mice ...

That night, Louisa wrapped the long, leather driving duster tighter around her body in a vain effort to keep the brisk wind at bay. She'd seriously have to re-think her Phoenix attire for the winter months. *Maybe there'll be less crime, and I won't be needed.*

Louisa huddled into the alcove closer to Morrie, but not too close.

A sharp click drew her attention down. Morrie, dressed as Hawk, pocketed his lock picking case somewhere on his person and opened the patent office door.

"Where did you put that thing? Your suit is skintight."

He chuckled. "I figured your first remark would be 'teach me how to do that,' not 'where do

I have my pockets.'"

"You'll teach me?" Her voice rose, hopeful.

"No."

"Then why offer?" Louisa closed the door behind them. Moon-shine filtered into the office, illuminating the space in bands of light.

"No, I didn't. I said I expected you to ask—never mind. You're being difficult." He scanned rows of filing cabinets that climbed chest high.

"So, then, where do you keep your pockets?"

He slapped the side of his thighs.

"Are you being cheeky with me?" Her gaze unwillingly traveled to his firm buttocks. *Is he teasing me?*

Morrie laughed. "I have pockets on the sides of my legs, my dear. They lie almost flat when nothing is in them and are just wide and deep enough for my usual tools. These, however"—he tugged at one of the two loops holding a small coil of rope by his hip—"were a necessary, recent addition to the uniform."

"*You* added—? Did you make that outfit?" Surprise bounced her words more than she intended.

"I did."

"You know how to sew?" But even as the words left her mouth, she shot a glance at her forearms. Of course he did; he'd sewn *her* back together, why not pieces of cloth?

He caught her looking at her arms and grinned before sliding open a wide drawer from one of the cabinets. Morrie riffled through the sideways files. Louisa leaned closer. Each sleeve held a master label marked ELECTRICAL ENERGY and was color-coded with either a blue, red, or green dot next to the patent title. Morrie pulled a thin sleeve out and opened it on top of the others in the cabinet. It was empty except for a large paperclip affixed to the top. He snapped the folder shut, slid it back in place, and closed the cabinet.

"What's wrong?" Louisa asked.

"It's still under assessment."

"And that means?"

He moved toward one of the back rooms. "It means they haven't determined the validity of it yet and are keeping it locked up until they know its worth. That's probably why the papers haven't heard about it. It's likely from outside Britain, too.

Maybe something from Bell in the Americas."

"Actually, Ryn did mention something about Bell."

"He can't seem to let the notion of sustainable electrical current go. Can you get a light?" He motioned to a small desk oil lamp as he lifted a stethoscope to his ears and kneeled before a safe the size of a kitchen cold box.

"You did not just take that out of one of your magic pockets," Louisa teased, still trying to see where the extra material was supposed to be. "Why on earth would you need a suit like this for anything other than secret crime fighting?" Louisa crouched beside Morrie, but he stiffened, and not from her nearness.

Without thinking, she placed a hand on his shoulder. "I'm sorry. Did I say something?"

He rolled his shoulder.

Louisa let her hand fall.

"When I was in the Americas, I ended up in New Orleans. I was supposed to be working for the white folks, helping out a well-known surgeon who worked in the area …"

"But?" she asked after a long moment.

"But I saw what was happening between them and the black folks, and I tried my best to help everyone. Well, that didn't work, and by the time the Battle of Liberty Place started, the Smiths had disavowed me. They'd apparently been on the confederate side of the civil war and became key supporters of the White League and their brethren. They didn't like me volunteering my time and expertise to the blacks."

Morrie had never revealed so much to her about his past. Louisa kept her breathing quiet and didn't say anything — didn't want to break the spell.

"We were trapped for days and desperately needed medical supplies. A reporter we'd been harboring told me where I could acquire some. We'd lost too many good men in the fighting, and so many more were injured. I couldn't ask them ... so I made this suit from scraps of leather. I had to hide my whiteness, blend in with the earth, and have freedom of movement to maneuver. I made this suit to help people. And that's the only reason I'm wearing it again." He lifted the stethoscope to the metal safe, near the combination lock.

Louisa opened her mouth to say something,

but Morrie put a finger to his lips and tapped his ear. They were done talking. Louisa remembered the newspapers covering the civil war and the subsequent micro-battles fought thereafter. Her mother made sure she'd kept abreast of international affairs during her studies. The Battle of Liberty Place had been three terrible days. But that was only two years ago. He must have come home shortly after. She still didn't know how he went from being a field medic to a reporter.

Joe's wise face, bearing only one good eye, popped into her head. He knew so much about fighting; about surviving ... and he had a distinctive southern Americas drawl. *I wonder if they met in New Orleans.*

A soft clunk resonated, and Morrie opened the safe. Louisa held the small lantern over his shoulder, illuminating the contents. *Morrie knows his way around this office a little too well ...* but he was a reporter and likely came by fairly regularly to follow up on the latest big idea for the newspaper. She was being ridiculous.

He shuffled through the three folders inside and drew one out that matched the empty file in the main records room. Morrie opened it on his knee to a blank page. He turned it over and flipped through the remaining sheets — all blank.

"Rapscallion!" he cursed and tossed it back into the safe, re-locking the device exactly as it had been. "Come on, we have to get out of here." He grabbed her hand and they ran back to the main door.

"Why? What's going on? Why was the file blank?"

He wrenched open the exit. Bug and Scythe stood waiting for them. Bug held some kind of new device that resembled a speaking-trumpet with a trigger.

"Now!" Scythe yelled.

A fine, shiny net flew out at them, expanding in the air.

Morrie slammed the door shut. "It's a trap! I knew something sounded off about that patent." He sprinted to the back of the building.

A spike of energy shot through Louisa's veins. Her heart hammered frantically against her ribs as she raced behind Morrie.

He bolted through a closet-sized door and up a back stairwell to a second floor, half the size of the offices below. Thousands of boxes lined floor-to-ceiling shelves. She and Morrie whipped up one aisle and along the far wall to a window.

Louisa helped him with the stiff sash. He climbed out first and clung to glopped mortar holds as he scaled the wall to the roof. Louisa followed, slower. Bug and Scythe's shouts filled the air.

When Louisa crawled over the roofline and scrambled to her feet, Morrie stood looking all around, a flurry of mental calculations marring his usually clear features.

"We'll have to jump." He pointed to the roof of the next building. It didn't look jumpable.

"Why don't we fight them?"

"With what? Your orbs distract and your gun extinguishes." He backed up, ran, and launched himself over the gap. Louisa didn't have time to think—she followed two steps behind, soaring in the air after him.

He stiffened.

Her lungs squeezed the breath from her.

He smashed into the opposite building, his upper body folding over the roofline a fraction of an instant before dropping. Morrie dangled, clinging to the edge with his hands.

Louisa landed firmly even as he scrambled against the wall, desperate for purchase. She whipped around and grabbed onto his wrists, braced her feet against the lip of the roof, and heaved. Morrie's hands wrapped around hers. His feet gained traction, and he stumbled up over the edge, crashing into Louisa. He pulled her into his chest as they stumbled and struggled to remain standing. His nose and lips nuzzled into her neck; her knees trembled. A scraping and scuffling echoed behind Louisa. Morrie's head jerked up.

"No!" He shoved her aside. The massive net enveloped Morrie. He collapsed to his knees, twitching and jerking and curling into a ball.

Scythe cackled. A great burst of energy rocked through Louisa. She smashed an orb at the thief's feet, knocking her back. Spinning around, Louisa shot Bug between the eyes with a wax practice round from the blunderbuss. With a whip-kick to Scythe's chest, Louisa used the momentum to twirl herself back to Bug, reloading with active rounds.

Fire spewed from the ever-ready launcher

strapped to his back, bathing the rooftop between them in heat and flame. Louisa staggered back from the inferno. She shot. Two deafening cracks broke the night. Bug stared at his now flameless-launcher.

Steel slid along steel. Louisa whirled around to face her nemesis. A glance at Morrie's still form lost Louisa her advantage. Scythe slashed at her. Louisa deflected one blade with the flared barrel of her gun and ducked beneath the other. Bug's launcher lit the sky again. The two thieves advanced, united.

Louisa jumped backward over Morrie and tried to pull the fine netting off him. An electric wave rode up her arm, chattering her teeth with just a finger's touch. She jerked away.

Head for the fire escape! Joe's voice.

No. I can't leave Morrie.

Run! I'm expendable. Morrie's words from the night of the masque.

He wasn't expendable, but he was right; then and tonight. She had to leave him or they'd capture her too.

A burning spread through her chest, and not from exhaustion. She parried the cutpurses' moves and slid down the metal ladder affixed to the opposite side of the building — the way Bug and Scythe must have gotten up.

Louisa ran into the night. She tucked in between a pair of row houses two streets over, trying to quieten her breathing to hear if they followed her. She risked a look around the corner of the house. Nothing moved. Louisa backtracked, but Big Ben rang out the hour, chiding her for being late. She had chaperone duty later that morning and had to sneak back into Bennett's place before anyone realized she was missing.

I can't leave him.

You can't save him.

I have to try.

And get caught? Everyone will know who you are, and then who will stop the Judge?

Louisa's insides churned, and she pulled at her duster, her skirt, her hair.

You know where they'll take him. Use that to your advantage. Now, go! You still have one more stop to make before home. No time to stand here and dither.

She had to go by the tavern. Joe would never forgive her for leaving Morrie behind, but he'd never speak to her again if she kept it from him. Either way, she'd failed them both tonight.

Chapter V
Deadly Celebrations

Louisa rocked back and forth on her heels, squeezing her hands together under the folded picnic blanket as yet another family walked past Bennett's group into Brompton Cemetery. The futility of waiting for a man she knew wasn't coming ate at her core. The hour approached elevenses.

"I guess he's not coming. Looks like you're right, Lou. Tweed must have his nose in a story." Bennett turned to Elenore; Mr. Arnold Digsby, Minister for Agriculture; and his lovely wife, Pricilla-Anne. He bowed low toward the grand north cemetery gate and picked up one of two baskets at his feet. Mr. Digsby collected the other, and the ladies led the group into the lush, wondrous grounds. Louisa trailed behind Mrs.

Digsby and Elenore.

Louisa had only ever picnicked here once before — with her mother. That was on All Souls' Day too; the only day Marie Pierce figured no one would look too closely and notice she wasn't of society anymore. Louisa barely acknowledged the grand lime trees lining the central avenue as Mrs. Digsby pointed out the most interesting headstones and statues along the path, marking a small sign of the cross in the air in respect for the deceased.

How could I have left him? How can I be here acting as if everything is normal when it's the furthest thing from the truth? What are they doing to him? Torture? And I left him. I left him. What's the matter with me?

No, I did what he told me to — what I had to do. Two against one wasn't going to work. I'm just learning to hold my own one-on-one. They would have overpowered me and then we'd both be hornswoggled. Gah! I need to fix this. And she would, but it would have to be after sundown.

That net had been meant for her. No one other than Ryn knew she had a partner. But thoughts of Ryn were no better. Louisa's friend had built the electrified net Bug used to capture Morrie. Louisa had stood in the same room with the engineer as she'd spoken about her father's next target.

It's a trap! Morrie's words echoed in her head.

"What say you, Lou?" Bennett asked, startling Louisa from her thoughts.

She glanced over her shoulder. "Pardon? I ... I was thinking about—"

"This Saturday, yes. I was just saying to Digsby that Elly really proved herself to those flying chaps we rounded up for her team. The Minis are in superb condition, aren't they?"

"Yes. Superb." Louisa gave a tentative smile to the gentlemen and resumed watching the cobbled walkway beneath her feet, brooding about her inability to save the one person that mattered the most to her. She caught her breath. Did she really mean that?

Bennett chuckled. "Don't mind Lou. We've had a lot on our plate this week. She's the only one who's kept me on track—even reorganized my desk for me yesterday. And wouldn't you know it, I can find everything now."

Louisa considered the absolute earliest time she could demand that Bennett and Elenore retire for the night. They'd be exhausted from all the fresh air this morning, and they had a full schedule set for the afternoon too. She could likely convince Elenore to head to bed early—maybe by nine o'clock, even. But Bennett never settled for the night before ten.

Can I sneak out before he goes down for the night? He'd be reviewing his speech and re-reading the final documents for submission—

"—you heard about anything so ridiculous, Lou?" Elenore asked.

Louisa blinked, caught off guard again. A group of children chased one another around the headstones. That was normal. Louisa had absolutely no idea what the women had been discussing.

"No, I haven't," she said, hoping it would be enough.

"Wait until I show you both," Mrs. Digsby prattled. "It is truly a sight. The myth goes that the key to Courtoy's mausoleum was lost shortly after Warner's death—he was working with Courtoy and Bonomi on the plausibility of temporal travel. Legend has it, he took the key with him the last time he used the mausoleum to travel through time and that's why no one can find it."

Some part of the lady's story triggered a memory deep inside Louisa. "Yes, but wasn't Warner considered a charlatan? I mean, he tried to sell technology to the military that was theoretically too advanced. It couldn't have been possible."

"But that in itself lends credence to the tale. His secret underwater weapon did blow up one ship during testing." Mrs. Digsby tapped the side of her nose knowingly. "You should see the Egyptian hieroglyphs banding the tomb, and its strange pyramidal roof. I tell you, Lady Courtoy knew what she was doing when she had it commissioned. And that was over thirty years ago."

The two ladies continued to gossip about the possibility of time travel as Louisa returned to plans for getting out of the house as early as possible. Problem was, even if she got Elenore to bed, Bennett would still be at his desk in the workshop for some time. *If I hid my Phoenix attire elsewhere … but where? And then there's still Courtright to contend with. I never know where she is at any given moment.*

"Hold up there," Minister Digsby called.

Louisa nearly walked into Elenore's back.

"It gets fairly crowded past the lower colonnade. There's a nice patch of sun over by that weeping willow. What say we set up there?"

Everyone was in agreement, so Louisa shook out the blanket, and the men spread it neatly near the tree. As they set up for tea, Marie Pierce's voice ran commentary in her daughter's head as Louisa took in her surroundings.

An anchor with a broken chain symbolizes the end of life. A broken column stands for a life cut short. A dove represents the transport of the deceased's soul …

Louisa nearly spilled her tea adjusting her legs into a more lady-like position even though she wore her usual slacks. The sun warmed the top of her head. Children laughed, running in and out of the far series of arches on the colonnade leading toward the chapel. But the nearby sculpted angel's face morphed into Morrie's, and again she witnessed his body twitch under Ryn's electric net until he'd given up and lain.

No one seemed to notice, or maybe they did but didn't mind her absentee thoughts, as the playful banter between Bennett and Elenore dominated the conversation. Louisa probably should have said or done something, but she knew they'd mostly behave themselves with the Digsbys around. She would return to protecting her charge's honor as soon as she got her partner back.

* * *

After cheerful goodbyes and fake air-cheek-kisses from Mrs. Digsby, the tea party separated back at the north gate.

"My goodness, would you look at the time." Bennett snapped his pocket watch shut and hurried over to Mrs. Abernathy's landau. Her man, Arthur, helped Elenore inside. She sat across from Bennett.

"Hold up there, Lou."

Louisa stopped, one foot on the side rail, her hands gripping the edge of the open door. She gave Bennett a quizzical look.

"I'm a mite concerned about Tweed. It's not like him to disappear. If he is on an extensive report or whatnot, can you check in with him at the newspaper and make sure everything is still a go for Saturday? I'm wondering about getting a backup documenter at this point." Bennett glanced at Elenore.

Something seemingly innocuous passed between them, but Louisa wasn't so sure. She didn't think they were trying to get rid of her for sly reasons. They had another engagement to attend within the hour—a lunch with a new potential backer for this project and maybe others down the road. Still, Louisa was certain they were colluding on something.

She blinked rapidly and stepped down again. "You want me to check on Mr. Tweed?" Of course, they didn't know he wasn't as the office ... or was he? Maybe he'd escaped after all, and she worried for nothing. Her head cleared fully for the first time all morning.

"Yes, sir. I'll check in with you after your appointment."

Bennett grinned. "Excellent. See you then. Okay, Arthur, home please."

The landau shuddered and sputtered, steam blasting, before jolting forward and finding its legs. Louisa turned in the opposite direction and walked to the West Brompton station.

On the ride to Northeast London, Louisa convinced herself three times that Morrie hadn't escaped and she was wasting time. That she needed to still tell Joe about what happened weighed heavily on her conscience. Then, three more times she rationalized the bar would still be closed, just as it had been at dawn, and there would be no Joe to speak to. At the very least, Louisa could verify that Morrie wasn't at work before coming clean to Joe about the incident.

But what if Morrie did escape? He's damn resourceful. Bug and Scythe can't watch him constantly. If they took that net off for even a few minutes so he could relieve himself, or eat, he'd know exactly what to do to get away.

Louisa practically ran the three blocks from Liverpool station over to the newspaper office on Middlesex Drive. The young woman behind the receptionist's desk recognized her and smiled, though she did tilt her head a smidge and squint at Louisa. Self-conscious, Louisa smoothed a few flyaway strands of hair, tucked them behind her ears, and straightened her frock coat.

"Good day. Would Mr. Morrison Tweed be available?" Even Louisa caught the note of desperation in her voice.

The pert-nosed receptionist hesitated a little too long. "Mr. Tweed is out on assignment. Would you like to leave a message?"

Louisa hated herself for asking, but she had to know. "Did he check in with the office this morning?"

The woman's gaze wavered slightly. She looked up and to the right. "It is not our policy to release information about the comings and goings of our reporters. Can't be too careful, you know. Is there anything else I can do for you?"

Louisa shook her head and turned away. This woman was being evasive and lying. Marie Pierce had not only taught her daughter how to behave in polite society but also how to spot any number of undesirable traits in others to ensure Louisa was never taken advantage of. But that meant Louisa couldn't walk out of there continuing to lie to herself about Morrie's safety.

The fifteen-minute walk to the tavern passed in a fog. Louisa almost got run over twice — once by a motorized cyclist and once by a horse. Though her stomach grumbled with the lack of food, not even the sausage vendor could draw her out of her brooding. The sun beat down from above, overheating her in no time, and bringing with it flashes of Bug's fire launcher.

Louisa had no idea how long she stood in front of the alley door leading to the basement salon, but the damp on her cheeks roused her back to the present. Deflated, she wiped the spilled tears and reached for the nob. A small spark of surprise jolted her heavy heart when it turned, before the self-loathing that had kept her awake all night returned.

Darkness ensconced the narrow stairwell, its shadows pushing at her from all sides as she clunked down the steps one at a time. At the bottom, she stared down the hall toward Morrie's preferred room. An ache flowed out of Louisa, through the closed bedroom door, and into the past. So many times he'd rescued her — saved her from herself — and she hadn't even been able to return the favor.

"Are ya gonna stand there all day or are ya comin' in?" Joe drawled from the main lounge.

Louisa dragged her heartache around the corner and into the tavern. The piano sat silent, yet an echo of its sad, sultry notes clung to the walls.

Joe dried a tub of glasses, slowly setting each cup in its place on the shelf behind the bar. He squinted at her.

"We're not open 'till six. We're not hirin' neither."

Reality slammed into Louisa hot and fast. *Morrie never told Joe my secret. He has no idea who I am.*

Leave.

No. He needs to know.

No. His dung-detector is better than mine.

She threw off her reservations, unpinned her hair, and shook out her wild curls. "Joe, I have bad news."

"Phoenix? D'at you?" The old southern black man set the glass and rag down on the bar top and leaned toward her.

"In the flesh, I guess."

"What's the matter?"

"I've failed you. You and Morrie."

"What are ya talkin' 'bout?"

"They've got him, Joe. Bug and Scythe. They were going after me and —"

" —he went 'n sacrificed hisself for ya."

"Uh … yeah. Got caught in their electrified net. It was a trap. For me. I … I couldn't fight both of them at once. I had to …"

"Get outta there right quick, I'm assumin'. So, what are ya goin' on 'bout failin' me for? You givin' up? Not goin' back? What?"

Her hackles rose. "No, I'm not giving up, but I don't know what to do. All my weapons and tricks, other than my hands and feet, are defensive. I need to go on the attack. Tonight. But I'm outnumbered, and I need something I can fight with that won't kill people but won't let them get close enough to hurt me."

Talking out the problem helped untangle her emotions and feelings of inadequacy. Her memory finally showed her something useful — the Steward walloping her derriere soundly with his walking staff the night of the masque.

"Like a long stick or a cane."

"Hmm … Yeah, a staff or bow would work well, but we don' have one; I don' know how to use one proper-like, and I can' find someone afore ya go after them *halfinch*. What about that gun o' yours?"

"Ryn!" Louisa sprang off the stool.

"That princess?"

"Yes. She's working on a project for me. New ammo. I'll have to stop by her place before I rescue Morrie. It just might give me the edge I need." She started for the door, pulling her hair back into a severe bun.

"Wait now. Don' go runnin' off so fast. There's summat here for ya." He removed an envelope from his breast pocket. "Found it stuffed under da door when I gots here. Couldn't understand why, but maybe I do now."

Louisa ripped open the letter bearing her night alias and read the tight angular cursive writing:

> *Back off or he dies.*
> *If you stay away this Saturday,*
> *he'll be released.*
> *If not, you'll get him back in pieces.*

They must have tortured Morrie into revealing a location she frequented. *Those rat bastards.* She looked up at Joe, eyes burning. "They'll regret they ever crossed me."

Chapter VI

Taking Names

Louisa listened the requisite three minutes outside the blackened conservatory, ready to rip Ryn a new one—*after* claiming her ammo. Anger and disbelief had boiled inside Louisa for the rest of the afternoon as she tried to figure out how Bug and Scythe were able to set a trap. The only answer that made any sense was *Ryn*. But the princess was volatile. If their interactions had proven anything, it was that the young woman always placed herself first.

A deep churning in Louisa's gut warned her even as her face grew hotter. Louisa burst into Ryn's workshop, startling the Indian princess hard at work on the opposite side of the table.

Hold it together, Lou. Get the ammo first. But the events of the last twenty-four hours ignited a frenzy within her.

"We've got a serious problem," Louisa snapped.

"And what might that be?"

"You've been compromised." Louisa stood up straight; the door banged close behind her. That wasn't what she meant to say, and yet the roiling in her guts lessened. Suddenly her unconscious musings caught up with reality and everything grew clear. They hadn't just set Shadow Phoenix up; they'd set Ryn up too.

"What are you talking about?" Ryn narrowed her eyes, put her project down, and crossed her arms.

"Your intel the other day. Your electrified net. It was a trap. Bug and Scythe knew I was coming. There was no patent, only a decoy. Tell me again, how did you learn about the hit?" Louisa pressed against the wide table and leaned forward on her hands.

"I overheard my father and his steward talking outside my door. They were discussing a letter, something his steward was to pen."

"Do they usually speak so?"

Ryn opened her mouth but no words came out. She blinked. "No. Usually I discover things quite by accident, and more often when I'm passing my father's study in the evenings. But how could they know?"

"The Steward, I bet. Remember the night he claimed you had 'rats' when I was hiding in your credenza—and you threatened to cut off his hands?"

Ryn nodded thoughtfully.

"I'd bet anything he told your father he suspected you weren't alone. Of course, the Judge would've dismissed it until he heard about me showing up at the museum. Then, at the masque, I think he was upset at you for more than sticking around and dancing with red-headed men. He must have seen you hug me. I could have been any random attendee, but he knows you" — Louisa caught herself before saying, *you have no friends* — "you like keeping to yourself. He likely has no idea that I followed Bug and Scythe to your door that night, but this hoax of a theft proves he was concerned enough to give weight to the Steward's warnings. They made sure you heard just enough to relay it to me. I showed up and now your father knows we've been working together.

"Ryn, I escaped but they got my partner. They're holding him hostage. They don't want me to interfere with whatever they have planned for the presentation on Saturday. I can't let them do this. Bennett's invention could end the drought. I need to save Hawk, too, but I also need your help one last time."

The engineer's eyes darkened at Louisa's ominous words. But it was true. If Ryn's father knew about their friendship, Louisa couldn't, in good conscience, put the princess at further risk.

"What do you need?" she asked, grim determination etched into every line of her face.

* * *

A bitter wind howled between the houses and shops along Pelham Crescent. Louisa gripped the slim, four-foot metal tube Ryn had bequeathed her in one hand; the other hand hovered over the hilt of her blunderbuss, still warm from her practice shots in the rail yard half-a-block behind her.

Louisa had packed all three sets of orbs: original, Ryn's, and smokescreen. She also wore her specialized arm guards along with her full Shadow Phoenix uniform. No one would catch her unawares tonight.

The shadows clung to her as she skirted from building to building along the semi-circle toward the cutpurses' lair. She searched around the establishment twice before crouching near the dark cellar window. Louisa focused on calming her pounding heart so she could listen beyond the glass pane into the room.

An owl hooted.

Hooves clopped.

Branches rustled.

But no sound came from inside.

No. This is too easy. It has to be another trap. They know I'm coming for him. Louisa waited another ten minutes and retraced her steps around the hideout. The shop above lay quiet and shut tight for the evening. Absolutely no light leaked out from any small space leading into the cellar.

I have to risk it. He would do it for me.

Louisa laid her pipe on the ground, pulled a screwdriver from her duster pocket, and shoved it between the windowpane and the frame. Her stomach cramped trying to keep the rampant butterflies in check.

The window popped open. Louisa expelled a slow breath and listened into the space beyond as she repacked her tool. She caught a waft of stale bread and mildew. Still, nothing moved beyond that simple barrier.

Louisa pushed the window up the rest of the way, set the stay, and eased backward through the narrow opening into the room. She grabbed her pipe before dropping the last few feet to the floor.

The silence weighed on her conscience. Was she too late, or had she gotten it all wrong? Louisa crouched low, the piece of metal resting across her knees, as she listened to the building breathe.

Nothing.

She stood up and shook one of her orbs. The static electric burst inside the sphere allowed it to glow for several seconds before dissipating. Using the faint light to see by, Louisa searched the entire lower floor — every rancid, ill-kept nook and cranny.

He's not here.

Not only that, but there was absolutely no

evidence to suggest he'd ever been there. *And where are Bug and Scythe? Out causing mayhem? No, not with such a high-value prisoner to watch over, surely?*

Louisa paced the entire basement a second time, her mind whirling.

So, then, where is he? Where did they take him? The Judge's estate?

No. They were forbidden and he wouldn't want any evidence linking him to the crime.

Another hideout?

Not likely.

Another associate?

Louisa halted and swallowed past the growing lump in her throat.

The Contessa.

"Those rat bastards." Fire and ice rocketed through Louisa's veins. *I have to find her.*

She slid the length of metal back out the window, then jumped up and crawled out, releasing the stay as she stood. Louisa reclaimed her new weapon and shot through the night-laden streets, avoiding officers on patrol, theater-goers, layabouts, and brightly lit roads.

Past the tavern door down the side alley, Louisa hopped the yard wall and let herself into headquarters — Morrie's place.

The dining room called to her. She had to find out everything there was to know about the Contessa — including where she stayed. Louisa flipped through the assortment of folders on the large table, glancing often at the bulletin board of sketches, the Contessa's face in particular.

She grabbed a thin file set away from all the others.

"There you are." Louisa dropped it flat before allowing her gaze to pull key words from the notes — a mix of typed and cursive. She pushed down a wave of panic at the familiar handwriting.

Focus!

The file covered everything about the Contessa: full name, her dead husband's family, the scandal surrounding his death, what ship she came in on, and even her weapons of choice. But nothing, absolutely nothing, about where she might be. Seven hotel cards had the word "no" scrawled across the back. That meant she was likely staying with someone in town. *But who?*

"Hellfire and damnation!" She slammed her hands down on the table, her curse echoing throughout the house.

I will not fail him.

Louisa had to concentrate. Who did she know in the social elite who might have an idea where to find the Contessa?

Only one name came to mind, and she'd already said goodbye. Louisa couldn't afford to place Ryn at any more risk—couldn't have her asking the wrong person for information …

And yet, who knew what those cutpurses were doing to Morrie? What would happen if Bug and Scythe were left to run loose during the cloud seeding presentation? Bennett and Elenore might lose everything. And what about the Queen? Rumor was, she attended major presentations.

Louisa shut the file on the Contessa, her mind made up. But she'd grabbed one folder edge too many and stared down at the man who'd nearly thrown her in jail. Morrie had been looking into him, had tracked his movements, and even made a schedule. It couldn't be coincidence her coming across his information twice in as many days.

What if I do fail? What if Ryn doesn't know how to track the Contessa?

Louisa scanned the calendar for Thursday and looked across to 11:00 p.m. Her heart gave a little leap. She scrambled back through the house and out into the blind alley.

* * *

Fog rolled thick off the Thames River and combined with the daily soot and grime of the city. Street lamps glowed like pale floss, barely illuminating the cobbles beneath Louisa's feet. An eerie quiet settled as she crouched in a darkened doorway, the occupants of the townhouse asleep for the night.

Footsteps echoed in the distance, seemingly from every direction, all the while getting closer. A tall figure wore a long, navy-blue frock coat, collar flipped against the cold, his head supporting a black bowler hat. The man walked past Louisa's doorway. She counted to ten and jumped down to street level.

"Inspector Hersh."

The policeman froze, his back to her. "Come to exact your revenge?" Hersh's nasally voice grated Louisa's sensibilities.

"Hardly." An anxious flood of energy pushed

an image of the Contessa slashing at Morrie to the fore of Louisa's mind. *I can't lose him.* She opened her mouth, ready to tell the inspector everything — but phantom flames from Bug's launcher incinerated the frantic urge.

Stick to the plan.

What plan?

Louisa sucked in a deep, fortifying breath. "Expect trouble at the Sky Port presentation on Saturday."

"I always expect trouble. Trying to place the blame for something on someone else again?"

"I told you, I'm not the bad guy. I'll be ... out of commission, but those two fiends your men keep letting get away have something big planned. Consider this a friendly warning — seeing as the Queen is expected to attend and all."

Hersh twisted around to confront the Phoenix, but she was already gone.

Chapter VII

When Life Gets in the Way

Marie Pierce appraised her daughter as the door of the asylum shut heavily behind them. "You look like death warmed over."

Both women gazed heavenward—Louisa to pray for the strength not to throttle her mother, and Marie to bask in the sun's warmth as a free citizen again.

The release hearing had been surprisingly brief. Louisa wouldn't have remained attentive much longer, anyway. She shifted Marie's single piece of luggage to the opposite hand and hailed a hansom cab—her mother had never been fond of technology and didn't trust the Steamies or *horseless carriages* as she called them.

If Louisa could, she'd learn to drive her own steam-powered landau. Too bad polite society frowned upon it. Her thoughts followed the well-worn path back to her second conversation with Ryn last night. Louisa automatically helped her mother up into the carriage.

Ryn had been a mixture of happy and irritated: Happy Louisa had changed her mind; irritated at almost losing her only friend. She didn't know much about the Contessa but had promised to send word the moment she discovered something useful.

Louisa plunked down beside her mother, the driver setting the heavy bag at their feet.

"Where to, ladies?" he asked before mounting the back of the snub-nosed carriage.

"Darlington's, please," Louisa said.

The driver hopped onto his perch, clicked his tongue, jiggled the reins, and joined the bustling streets guiding them to the well-known fabric and dress shop

"I was beginning to wonder if you would make me interview with the poor excuse for a wardrobe you left me."

Louisa eyed her mother. She looked considerably healthier now, but still only a shadow of the woman she had once been — except for the opinionated commentary. That was as strong as ever.

"Mr. Bennett asked me to take you shopping — his treat as a welcome home gift."

Marie's eyes glittered, making her appear a lot like her old self.

"He is a single young man who is far keener on the latest invention than what is in fashion. He gave me £10. You can purchase thirty yards of fabric, and I'll help with a good — "

" — pair of boots. Yes, I know the price of cloth, Louanna."

"Louisa. Louisa Wicker. And you are?"

Her mother frowned. "Mary Wicker, widow."

"Exactly. Louanna doesn't exist and neither does Marie anymore. From scratch, remember?"

"I don't need to be scolded like a schoolgirl, you know. I am still your mother."

Louisa closed her eyes and leaned her head back against the cushioned leather seat. She didn't need this aggravation right now. Her head grew heavy, but just before she could doze off, Morrie shoved her, shouting, "It's a trap!" She jerked awake. Morrie hadn't pushed her, Marie had.

"It's impolite to sleep when you're acting as an escort. The least you could have done was get some rest before collecting me."

Louisa bit the inside of her cheek and pressed her fingernails into her palms. The tricks Miss. Margaret had shown her for combatting unwanted amorous feelings worked just as well against anger and frustration. Louisa had to remain calm. Advising her mother that she spent her nights searching for her male crime-fighting partner and dealing with a pig-headed police inspector bent on tossing her in jail was not what she had in mind for a conversation with her no-longer-insane mother.

The cab pulled up to the curb alongside Darlington's Fine Fabrics, and the driver helped the women down.

"I'd like to hold the cab, please. We have a couple of errands to run with a final stop at the station." Louisa handed the man a small incentive to stick around.

"Certainly, ma'am. Be right here when you're done." He tipped his tweed cap and stepped up to speak with his horse.

Marie raised an eyebrow at her daughter and led the way into the shop. Louisa browsed the latest fashions worn by the dress forms as her mother inspected bolts of cloth. A golden sari, trimmed in red, sat tucked in the corner. Ryn, working on some un-named mechanical project, flashed to mind. Louisa still couldn't believe the girl's own father had used her to set a trap for Shadow Phoenix. And Morrie had sensed something was off from the start. If Louisa hadn't been so damned adamant, Ryn wouldn't have been exposed as a double-agent, and Morrie wouldn't have been captured and held for her cooperation.

" —isa? Louisa, dear, I'm ready now."

Louisa shook her head to clear it, tried a deep breath, but coughed instead. She abandoned the lonely sari and paid for her mother's purchases.

Outside, they left the parcel of cloth with the cabbie and walked up the street to the cobbler. The chimes above the door jangled. Marie clasped her hands as she surveyed the offerings in her size. The store owner, Mr. Shoer, completed a sale and hurried over from behind the counter. Marie's eyes lit up. She was about to say hello when Mr. Shoer gave her a polite nod and opened his arms in welcome to Louisa.

"Miss. Wicker, what a lovely surprise. How are the new boots treating you?"

"They're perfect, thank you."

"What brings you fine ladies to the store today?" He glanced from mother to daughter, unaware who stood before him.

"Marcus, I'd like you to meet my mother. She is just returned from Egypt." A knowing look passed between Louisa and the shopkeeper. It was common for women taken ill, often of severe vapors, to visit a warmer climate until their health returned.

Her mother offered a hand. "Marie—"

"Mary Wicker, widowed," Louisa said.

Mr. Shoer had known Marie Pierce when she had perfect porcelain skin, strawberry blonde hair, and a heavy purse. The anemic, sallow faced, auburn-haired woman before him was unrecognizable.

"My mother requires a sturdy pair of daily shoes. She is a governess and will likely be on her feet much of the time. It is a prominent household, so something with a hint of the latest fashion would be preferable."

Mr. Shoer bowed over Marie's hand and released it. He gave a quick smile and pulled down three pairs of footwear — two styles of shoe and one pair of walking boots.

Louisa's mother didn't move. Her daughter read the disbelief and hurt reflected in her eyes. She held her mother's shoulders lightly and guided her to a bench to try on the footwear. Mr. Shoer treated Marie as he did any other customer — like a cousin of the Queen. He loved his job and took pride in helping others, but he clearly didn't remember who she used to be.

As Louisa scanned the shoes and boots on display, she knew which ones the cobbler had made and which ones were built through traded labor. It was in the stitching. Novices didn't have enough time, in one night, to double stitch all the areas that wore down faster. That, and the price. Two pairs of size twelve riding boots looked nearly identical except for the stitching and the resulting lower price of the less qualified craftsmanship. Louisa thought for a moment of the man in the alley she'd stopped from stealing boots. It was hard to believe that had been over a month ago. She hoped he'd taken her advice.

Marie chose the ankle boots, better for walking in dresses, and Louisa paid the humble cobbler, making sure to tip him well. He had once given her a pair of dancing shoes for trade, and she'd since borrowed leather for her Phoenix mask from her old, sturdy boots. He knew very well who she was and was always happy to see her.

Marie remained quiet on the short ride to the train station. She watched, detached, as Louisa did and said all the things Marie had taught her daughter to do and say ... all the things that once fell on her shoulders.

Louisa regarded her mother carefully and continued to study her on the trip south to Clapham. The doctor who oversaw Marie's stay at the asylum had taken Louisa aside as Marie collected her belongings after the hearing. He was hopeful regarding her continued recovery, but concerned. The first forty-eight hours would be crucial to setting the tone for her reintegration into society.

Louisa gave an inner sigh and massaged her forehead as she looked out the window, the city trundling by. She struggled to think clearly. Too much was at stake—too much to figure out between Morrie's capture, Bennett's presentation, and now her mother's release. There was nothing she could do about the men right now; she could not be Shadow Phoenix while the sun shone. But, as Louisa Wicker, she could help ease her mother's transition.

"I know it's short notice, but Mr. Bennett's neighbor, the widow I spoke with you about?"

Marie drew away from the scenery and focused a sharper gaze on her daughter. "Yes."

"She invited us to tea this afternoon." Louisa held up her hand to stay her mother's words. She hated lying, but Marie needed something substantial to grasp onto. "It is not an interview. She wishes to welcome you home after your time abroad. There will be no talk of the available position and no vying to prove you are the better candidate. Do you understand? Just tea."

"Is she holding tea with any of the other governesses?"

"Not that I'm aware of, why?"

"My dear, as well-rounded a young woman as you are, there are still things your mother can teach you. This is a pre-assessment. She obviously sees me as a potential candidate and would like to evaluate me under social conditions to make sure we get along well and that my pedigree stands up to scrutiny. Politics, Louann—Louisa. There's always a hidden agenda."

Louisa gaped at her mother.

"Close your mouth, it's unbecoming." She eyed her travel dress critically. "This afternoon you say? Well, that certainly won't give me enough time to fashion a respectable dress. I'll have to see what I can do with the few articles of clothing you saw fit to leave me with."

"We're not so different in size. You can borrow from my wardrobe."

Marie's critical gaze zipped from the crown of Louisa's head, where Louisa felt stray curls wisp down, to her shoulders, bodice, slacks, and boots.

"I do own more than a dress or two, Mother. These are my new work clothes. I needed something maneuverable. As an inventor's assistant, skirts are cumbersome and restrictive." In fact, Louisa had left most of her day-dresses at the boarding house, so there'd be plenty of selection, even if her mother frowned upon a hand-me-down gown.

"We'll see. Tell me about the widow and the children."

The old cunning spark was back in Marie's eyes and only grew stronger the longer the women spoke of the coming tea and their hostess. After a short walk from Clapham station to the Applewood Apartments, Louisa juggled her mother's bag and parcels without complaint — out loud, anyway.

At the door, Miss. Margaret welcomed Marie like a long-lost sister. With traces of flour dust whitening the hair at her temples, Margaret removed her apron and immediately started the tour — first stop, the kitchen. Louisa placed her mother's things at the bottom of the stairs.

"Oh, Louisa" — Margaret glanced over her shoulder — "a letter arrived for you this morning. It's on the odds-and-ends table in the parlor by the fire."

A letter?

Louisa's heart jumped. She hurried into the next room and stopped short before the small round table. A white envelope sat propped against a delicate porcelain vase. Beneath the envelope lay the morning's paper. Louisa couldn't help it; she scanned the front page for Morrie's bi-line. Nothing. Not even the piece he'd been working on about the airship inspection. The all too familiar ache rose in her chest. She managed a deep shuddering breath and picked up the envelope:

> *L. Pierce*
> *Applewood Apartments*
> *7 Chip Street, Clapham*

Louisa tore it open and scanned the one-page message, which spoke of nothing more significant than the weather. But it was signed by R. Tamberlain—a salute from Ryn, acknowledging that Louisa had not given her the full truth about whom to address her findings to.

And this was no ordinary letter. Louisa's mother had received many such seemingly innocuous letters from wives requesting assistance with their husbands' loyalties. It was a classic hidden message. She just had to figure out which method.

"Here, let me help you with these," Margaret said, her voice filtering into the parlor. The accompanying rustling emphasized the tour moving up to the next floor.

At a glance, Louisa knew it wasn't an acrostic pattern. The one her mother relied on most often had been the first letter of each sentence that added up to spell a word; new paragraphs signified new words. She gathered the corresponding letters together in her mind.

She gasped.

Louisa had expected a challenge … but not this.

* * *

My dear,

It has been too long since we last corresponded. The days here remain stretched and the skies clear. At least the lack of rain has made travel easier, though I do not venture out much anymore. Last week, my father held a masquerade for all the usual elite. It served as a wonderful occasion to present myself since no one else was going to, and I've been eighteen for several months now. A whirl around the dance floor made for a delightful break from the ordinary. Notwithstanding, the bold move likely gave my father heart palpitations!

Evenings remain the hours I cherish best. Most nights I find myself taken with a new project, a new distraction. But I digress. As always, I speak too much of myself. Surely, your days are far livelier. Should you need a diversion toward the mundane, however, do think of me. Your friend,

R. Tamberlain

Louisa shifted over to the common writing desk and scratched out the message:

Italian Embassy

EPISODE VIII
Trifecta

Chapter I

Social Torture

"Really, I don't see why we have to walk." Marie Pierce gripped her parasol tighter as the wind threatened to relieve her of it.

Louisa sighed—something she did far too often in her mother's company.

"It's a simple walk. I'm not made of money." Louisa led the way along Bennett's street past the Commons, following the route she used to take to get from the Applewood Apartments to the townhouse.

"You could have fooled me. Train rides, cabs, you even bought my boots." Marie admired the fashionable footwear as she walked. "I saw you tip the cobbler."

"We're supposed to, Mother. *You* taught me that."

"And he was altogether too friendly with you. What if another customer had seen?" She still wasn't over the fact that Mr. Shoer hadn't recognized her. Louisa's mother was having trouble adjusting to life as Mary Wicker—though, it had been less than a day. Louisa tried to give her mother the benefit of the doubt, but she wasn't making it easy.

"It's this one, here." Louisa indicated the Abernathy residence with a wave and turned up the walkway. She reached to ring the bell.

"You're not going to present yourself like that, are you?" Marie's exacting gaze sliced the air from Louisa's head to her boots.

Louisa narrowed her eyes and pulled the cord connected above the widow's doorframe. "What are you talking about?"

"Your hair's come loose, you're slouching, and the wind has rumpled your frock." Deft hands smoothed and straightened every possible aspect of Louisa's appearance.

She tried to swat her mother away, but nothing less than the door opening stopped the woman.

"Ah, Miss. Wicker, right on time. Do come in."

Arthur, Mrs. Abernathy's houseman, bowed.

"Mr. Cline, it's lovely to see you." Louisa handed him her coat, a task she used to perform not that long ago. "I'd like to introduce you to my mother, Mrs. Mary Wicker. Mother, this is Mr. Arthur Cline, Mrs. Abernathy's steward."

He chuckled. "Don't know as I've ever been called that before, but yes, I'm her man. Pleased to meet you." He hung Marie's frock in the closet and set her parasol, really Louisa's from her childhood, by the front entrance. "This way, ladies. The missus will be in shortly. She likes to peek in on the little ones 'bout this time of day."

Arthur led them to a bright parlor with a cheery fire. The women sat in two of the plush high-backed chairs. Louisa kept her posture straight, shoulders back, chin at just the right angle so as not to disrespect but not to submit either. Her mother was watching, after all. But when all of her old etiquette lessons fell quiet, two words invaded her mind: *Italian Embassy*.

Princess Brynna Tamberlain Fitzhugh had miraculously come through for Louisa, embedding the secret message in an inconspicuous letter.

Those two words provided the solution to her desperate search for Morrie when she'd failed to find the captured journalist at the thieves' hideout. They represented not only hope and certainty but also the impossible.

"Louisa, dear, how wonderful you and your mother could make it." Abernathy bustled into the room, her eyes alight with joy.

Louisa and Marie stood to greet her.

"You must be Mrs. Wicker." The widow shook hands with Marie.

"Please, call me Mary. It's lovely to meet you. Louisa speaks highly of you. Thank you for the invitation to tea."

"My pleasure. And please, it's Patricia. I thought after your extended stay abroad you might enjoy a little hometown comfort."

Marion, the maid Mrs. Abernathy now shared with Bennett since Louisa's promotion, carried in a silver platter replete with tea, cups and saucers, and mini cucumber sandwiches. She curtsied, raised an eyebrow at Louisa, and then departed.

What was that about? Louisa absently fixed her hair and smoothed out her vest and slacks.

"You're very thoughtful. Yes, I'm certainly happy to be home."

"Louisa mentioned you'd been under the weather."

Louisa eyed her mother to make sure she didn't stray from the script.

"Yes, a bad bout of the vapors. Louisa convinced me some time away might do me good. So, I contacted an old university friend who'd left me with an open invitation to visit."

Louisa relaxed her spine … a little. Her mother behaved, even if she'd found a way to get in a dig about her "time away."

Italian Embassy … Louisa blinked. She couldn't give over to her thoughts. She had to stay vigilant. Present. Sure, her mother had promised not to make more of this tea than what it was, but she'd promised Louisa a lot of things growing up — most of which had been lies.

" — tells me what a life saver you've been these past months." The widow looked at Louisa as the matron poured the tea.

Codswallop. I drifted.

"Oh?" She figured that was a good, neutral

response, and smiled.

Abernathy addressed Louisa's mother. "Of course, she won't admit it, but I must say, since your daughter and Andrew have been working together that young man has really come alive."

Louisa blushed.

Abernathy patted her on the hand. "Now, dear, I don't mean to imply anything. I know he has a soft spot for that young pilot staying with him, but you've been like a sister. In fact, you're about the same age as Bethany — or the age she would have been." The widow sighed dramatically.

Marie leaned in. Gossip was in the air.

"After the poor dear passed — she had consumption, you know — Andrew dedicated himself to his studies. Became something of a hermit. His older brothers are both busy lads, but the few times they visited they couldn't get him out of his funk. You know, his middle brother is a pilot with the Royal Air Force, and the eldest is in banking. Took over the family business ..."

Louisa hadn't known about Bennett's sister, though he had mentioned his brothers in passing. He must have recognized some aspect of Bethany in her. He'd been so familiar with her from the start. And then asking her to help him with the cloud seeding project — why, he must have transferred his trust for his sister to her. He'd needed someone to share this with.

"Of course, being the youngest son, Andrew has the hardest stretch to prove himself. As you know, the first son follows the father, and the second son goes into the military. If a family has the luxury of having a third son, he really must strike out to make it on his own." Mrs. Abernathy collected another sandwich.

"Indeed, 'tis the way of things. But it sounds as though Mr. Bennett is well on his way to being a respected engineer ..." Louisa's mother took the conversation and ran with it.

Yes, Bennett's cloud seeding patent was poised to make history. Why the Judge wanted to back Sterling's inferior design made no sense. Just more back-room politics, to be sure. The visages of the Judge's two main flunkies warred for prominence in Louisa's head: Bug's short stature and grim features against Scythe's sharp, lanky form. The two meant to sabotage the presentation to the

Society of Engineers tomorrow. She couldn't let them. Bennett had come to mean just as much to her as she did to him ...

Morrie.

Those villains had Louisa's partner — would only let him go if she backed off; if she put the reporter's well-being above Bennett's. A violent ache threatened to shred her heart.

I have to find Morrie.

This would not come down to Louisa having to choose one over the other.

Italian Embassy.

Ryn had given her the key. The only other place the cutpurses could be holding Morrie was with the Contessa — and the Contessa currently sojourned at the Italian ambassador's residence and place of business.

A youthful peal of laughter and a light-hearted squeal carried into the parlor from the hall, breaking Louisa's musings.

"Children, present yourselves," Mrs. Abernathy boomed.

The giggles ceased and a young miss and master with corn-silk hair stood resolutely, side-by-side, in the doorway, eyes downcast.

"My, how the time flies. Today's lessons must be over. Children, come here."

The pair walked in synch, like little automatons, to stand before their great aunt.

"Mary, Louisa, these are my niece's children—Camille and her younger brother Peter."

Camille curtsied. Peter bowed.

"Missus"—Marion popped her head into the room—"sorry to interrupt, but there's something amiss with the jelly."

"Oh, heavens, please excuse me." The widow rose and swept from the room. "You haven't let it boil too long, have you?"

The children stood like statues. The only movement Louisa detected was from Peter's eyes. Marie caught it too. Louisa held her breath, waiting for the standard beratement and lesson in manners.

But it never came.

Her mother followed the boy's gaze across the room to the baby grand piano sitting silently by the front window.

"Something caught your eye?" Marie asked in a soft, playful tone.

Louisa stiffened. *She'd* never been spoken to like that in her life — at least not by Marie Pierce.

The boy bit his lip and looked down when his sister nudged him, almost imperceptibly, with her elbow.

"Don't be shy, now." Marie stood and walked over to the shiny black piano. "Why don't you join me?" She pulled the bench seat out, settled in the middle, and raised the fallboard. With one finger, Marie gently plunked out the tune to *Mary Had a Little Lamb.*

Slowly, the boy abandoned his post beside his sister and shuffled over to the piano. Marie patted the bench beside her, then with two fingers played Chopsticks.

"Would you like to help me?" Marie asked.

Peter sat and nodded.

She plunked out the melody in the upper register

He tried it.

"Now, you play at the same time as me. Ready?" And the two of them played, blending seamlessly. The boy had an ear. Well, that was all the incentive little Camille needed. Before Louisa could finish blinking, the girl sat on the other side of Louisa's mother, learning the melody in the lower register.

By the time Mrs. Abernathy returned, the three of them played the tune together.

"Brava! Brava!" The widow clapped.

The children blushed and jumped to standing. Even Louisa jolted, so engrossed that she hadn't seen their hostess return. Marie closed the fallboard and swung around.

"You have a pair of gifted children here, Patricia. You must be very proud."

"To the kitchen, my dears. Your tea awaits." Mrs. Abernathy encouraged the children with a wave toward the door, and they complied.

The widow resumed her seat across from Louisa, and Marie rejoined them.

"Honestly, I had no idea. Their studies don't include the arts. Though I really should rectify that. I do believe my niece saw to their education of all things refined. Did you see little Peter's face as he played? No, of course not, you were instructing Camille at the time. I tell you, pure joy simply radiated from the boy. I've never seen the pair so entranced. You've given me much to think about."

Louisa didn't want all this roundabout praise getting to her mother's head. The expression on Marie's face was a familiar one—calculating. Louisa had warned her not to read too much into this visit, but she'd gone and turned it into an opportunity to show off. Louisa changed the subject.

"I do hope everything is all right with the jelly."

Chapter II

Stakeout—Hold the Béarnaise

The only good thing about the change in season was the chance to sneak out of the house sooner with an earlier nightfall. The problem with having Louisa's plans go her way, though, meant more people on the streets—and the cover of dark could only do so much. Luckily, the prominent neighborhood of Eaton Square was less frequented at this hour, or so the clerk had implied. Therefore, the obstacles before her were avoiding Buckingham Palace, staying off Palace Road, and avoiding shop owners and the elite on their way home on Ebury Street as she made her way to Lower Belgrave.

Louisa slipped between two large houses across from where Chester Square met Lower Belgrave and stared at Italian Ambassador Luigi Federico Menabrea's office and residence. Two porch lights illuminated a figure in trim blues holding a rigid stance at the bottom of the short flight of stairs. Because he was back-lit, Louisa couldn't make out any of his finer features, but the cut of his jacket and decided lack of a billy, stovepipe or those newer tall helmets meant he wasn't a *peeler* — of the local constabulary. That also meant he was a complete mystery as far as his training and weapons went.

"Better not cross him."

She shifted to slip across the street in the darkest spot between two lampposts, but the guard checked his pocket watch and then slowly paced around the exterior of the house. Louisa held her position and watched. Would a new guard rotate from the back to the front? Would one exit the main door and take up the abandoned post? She'd drilled Ryn on everything the Indian princess knew about embassies in the brief time she had before heading over.

Louisa's gaze flickered from the yard's trees to the right side of the house, over to the left, up the street, down the street, and back to the porch. Eventually, the guard circled 'round from the opposite side and stood in the exact location as before.

Louisa couldn't be certain it was the same guard, so she marked the angle of his fedora and small, bright scuff on the toe of his left shoe. She also retrieved her own pocket watch from her work pouch, noting the time. Her heart pummeled her chest even as her stomach knotted and undid itself.

She had to do this right. This wasn't the Contessa's permanent residence; it was the Italian Ambassador's. He likely had no idea what her dark hobbies were ... or maybe he did. Louisa groaned. Regardless, she was doing the very thing Morrie warned her not to — breaking the law.

The guard glanced at his watch in an almost identical manner as before and paced toward the side of the house. Louisa glanced at the hour. Twelve minutes had passed. When he returned, she marked the time again: seventeen minutes. And it was the same guard.

She watched him, tracking his movements for three-quarters of an hour. He stood at the front for ten to fifteen minutes and took between fifteen and twenty minutes to canvas the property around back before returning to his front post.

Louisa waited five minutes after his next round started before darting across the street and stepping into the shadows of the side yard — a good fifty feet between the grand houses. She crouched behind a small clump of shrubs, closer to the adjoining property, but with an unobstructed view of the rear yard. And the guard stood there for his usual ten to fifteen minutes.

So, he spends little time on the side yards. Once he passes, I'll have maybe twenty minutes to find a way in. But he might hear me. She abandoned that idea. No, she'd have to use the ten-minute window of time when he re-stationed himself at the front. That way, he'd be less likely to detect her with the greater distance between them.

As she waited, Louisa assessed the house itself. At three stories, a widow's walk surrounded a smaller attic space with octagonal windows but held no obvious entry point — decorative only. Which meant the wrought-iron fencing likely attached directly to the roof and not to an actual walkway.

The guard rotated back to his front position.

Louisa kept low and moved to a bush with a better view of the back of the house.

Over the next thirty minutes, Louisa determined the best way in would be via the roof. The back door was locked. A soft light flickered behind the drapes, indicating someone was still up in the main portion of the house. None of the second or third-floor windows were cracked open—too cold. Even then, they'd likely lead to occupied guest rooms and servants' quarters. The same held true for all the lower windows. The only way in was top down.

Louisa removed the narrow pipe Ryn had permitted her to take the other night and laid it on the ground. She didn't have a proper holster for it, and it might fall at any time. The guard came 'round. She waited for him to leave again. Her heart and stomach continued to pull in opposite directions—one wanting to burst in and find Morrie, the other plummeting to her feet at the prospect of breaking and entering the domicile of an Embassy representative. If she got caught … No, she couldn't think like that.

The guard disappeared around the corner of

the house, and Louisa scuttled out from behind the shrub. She scaled the aged oak close to the building. Half the oak's leaves still clung to its sturdy branches, but she climbed the tree with care — a fair number of acorns fell. The farthest she could go without threat of damaging the oak was level with the third floor. She nestled in close to the trunk on the last of the limbs that could bear her weight, and she waited.

Don't even think of rushing this.

If Louisa tried to scale the remaining height of the house right now, she'd get caught for sure. Tonight was not a night for impatience. Morrie had to escape. She couldn't afford to mess this up. Everything was at stake. The solidness of the trunk pressed between her shoulder blades helped ground her as the heavy perfume of dewy, half-decomposed leaves overwhelmed her. She stifled a cough.

Louisa studied the brickwork, glad of the half-ledge made by the masons along the window ledge line below the roof. Even the windows popped out from the flat wall and sported mini-roofs — dormers. Her gaze tracked the ideal path from branch to ledge to window to roof.

Fallen leaves rustled. The stoic guard returned, ever vigilant.

Louisa couldn't concentrate with the man standing below her, not a stone's throw away. It didn't help that, this close, the darker stripe crossing his chest was not the sash she'd suspected. The supple leather did not form a knot at his hip, but a holster—and the gun was three times the size of the Contessa's Derringer.

She swallowed, trying to force down the lump in her throat. For some reason, Bug's fire launcher, and even Scythe's blades, didn't affect her quite the way a gun did. Her modified blunderbuss didn't count. Even with Ryn's new ammo, the weapon wasn't lethal. Just last night, Louisa and the engineering princess had experimented with all the options her friend had developed. But the discovery that the cutpurses hadn't taken Morrie back to their hideout had stripped Louisa emotionally raw. It was her turn to save him, and she hadn't even known where to find him. She still didn't.

Louisa was about the break into the Italian

Embassy on a hunch. A hunch that Bug and Scythe had been commanded to retain the Contessa's help. Even if she was helping the thieves, it wasn't necessarily from the Contessa's temporary place of residence. But Louisa had nothing else to go on. She had to believe Morrie was here—it was the only thing keeping her sane.

Ten minutes ticked by. Louisa didn't have her watch out, but she knew. *He's not leaving.* Her breath caught and her pulse quickened. *Hold it together. His internal clock isn't as precise as yours.* Sure enough, three minutes later he checked his watch and turned to leave. Louisa slumped against the tree. Her weight shuddered the branches of the limb. A handful of acorns tumbled to the ground.

He turned sharply and kneeled. One hand reached for a nut and the other for the revolver hilt. He held an acorn and looked up.

Louisa froze.

He searched the dark, half-barren tree.

She swallowed. If Louisa could see him, the reverse was also true. She held her breath.

His gaze settled right on her.

Bloody hell. She tensed, ready to launch herself

on the bloke from three stories up.

A steam landau shuttered by out front, coughing for lack of coal. The guard turned his head away. The noise faded.

Louisa's lungs burned from lack of air, and her muscles ached from being simultaneously cramped and ready for action.

An owl hooted. Something small scrabbled through the leaves. The guard dropped the nut, rose, and walked around the far side of the house.

Louisa waited a full five minutes before moving. She had to be sure he didn't double back. A burst of wild energy jolted through her. She scrambled out onto the limb and hung from it, suspended over the ground and swung her body back and forth, the tree groaning slightly. Mid up-arc Louisa let go and soared toward the solid brick wall. She slammed into it, scrabbling to grip the small decorative edge — a corbeled rowlock. Louisa blinked to get rid of the nonsense information. Her fingers ached as she struggled to hold tight.

Come on. You can do it. For Morrie.

She raised her leg and caught the toe of her boot on the ledge, spider-walking the other leg, heel-to-knee, along the biting brick until she hauled her body up. Louisa balanced on both feet, chest against the wall, and slid along. Her heart raced. Sweat beaded across her brow.

Horses sweat, Ladies glow, her mother chided. Louisa gritted her teeth and reached for the dormer, clambering up onto its mini-roof.

Go, go, go!

She was out of time.

Louisa crouched on the small peak and jumped. Cold iron dug into her hands as her body landed hard against the main roof. A crunch came from her sphere pouch, but she couldn't think about that now. Louisa pulled her body up the wrought-iron fence and dropped onto the other side. She lay there, squished between the fence and the roof of the fake widow's walk.

A hysterical sob threatened to bubble out. She concentrated on her breathing. Louisa stared up into the night and listened to the scrape of the guard's footsteps. After another twelve minutes of relative silence, a steady grind announced the continuance of his route.

Louisa heaved herself up and examined the

octagonal, mullioned window. It didn't open. She pushed past the growing tightness in her chest and duck-walked around the attic vent. Louisa dug her fingers around the edges, but it was sealed tight. She might not have her pipe or most of her lightning orbs, but she did have her screwdriver.

In no time, Louisa loosened the fasteners and pried the vent away from the roof. She looked inside but couldn't see much. Louisa fumbled in her pouch through shattered bits and loose powder to find two spheres still intact. She shook one. The faint illumination revealed boxes, trunks, and old wardrobes — nothing more. However, the resulting hole was a tad small. She eyed it critically, removed her long coat, and stuffed it through the opening before doing the same with herself.

Chapter III
Olly, Olly Oxen Free

*A*ttics *creak … it's what they do.* Louisa alternated the syncopation of her steps. Between that and the slight wind whistling through the eaves, it should be enough not to draw attention to herself. Still, her chest ached with the constant tension. The guard almost caught her — someone else might too.

Louisa tugged the door at the top of the stairs. It didn't budge. She nearly pulled herself into it. *Codswallop.*

Is it locked? She shook her orb. The dim light illuminated the knob. *No keyhole. Just stuck.* She blew strands of hair out of her face. *Okay, where's it jamming?* Louisa inspected the frame, noted where the gaps were, the directionality …

Ah ha.

She lifted the door by the handle, shifted the

top more left than straight, and pulled. It popped open. Her stomach rocketed up and plummeted down as fast as a child's ball.

Louisa breathed deeply, calming her heart rate so she could listen beyond the noise of her own body. Nothing. Carefully closing the door behind her, Louisa considered the steep, narrow stairs descending before her. Each step presented too many possibilities to alert the household of her presence — so she'd eliminate them all.

She climbed onto the baseboards lining either side of the stairs, the straddle unladylike but not uncomfortable. Louisa pressed her palms against the walls and shimmied her way down to the third floor without ever touching a step.

At the bottom, she listened for the telltale signs of the servants settling in for the night: water poured into dry sinks, wardrobe doors shutting, the creak of bed-boards, and the clatter of night rituals. Either everyone was already settled, or this was a late-run household. Usually, at this time of night, only Isabel, Bennett's cook, and Courtright, his housekeeper, were up.

But if the Contessa is staying here, she's likely to

have a personal maid or attendant. Even if the servant had been sent to bed for the night, she wouldn't sleep until she knew the Contessa had settled. That meant quiet did not equal safe.

Louisa stepped into the corridor and headed down the hall for the servants' back stairs, keeping close to the walls with less risk of noise from the floorboards.

She slipped out of sight into a stairwell just wide enough for a single servant. Surprisingly, the damask pattern lining the walls was pale with a slight texture. Usually, back stairs were void of even such simple luxury. Maybe it was an Italian thing.

Louisa hurried down the thinly carpeted stairs when a repeating clunk echoed up from the first floor.

Blast! Do I retreat or push on? Ryn had mentioned the protocol for such places. While the princess had never set foot in an Embassy or any other society function beyond the walls of her own home, her ears worked just fine.

The Contessa might have a bodyguard in addition to her attendant, and the ambassador likely had one as well.

With Morrie's life at stake and the current stairway-odds in her favor, there was no going back. She hurried to the open hall of the second floor and flew through the first door on the right, not quite closing it behind her. Louisa leveled her quick breaths and placed her ear next to the crack. A servant padded up the stairs, steadily climbing to the third floor.

Louisa glanced around the dim, musty space. The overwhelming abundance of sage hues in a mix of bold patterns on tapestries, bed drapes, coverlets, carpets, and walls lent validity to the brass plaque she'd glimpsed on the outside of the chamber door: *Stanza Verde.*

Her mother had made Louisa study languages as well as culture and etiquette growing up, and while she'd easily get lost in most conversations besides English and French, she could read German, Spanish, and Italian just as well as any lady might.

When all was quiet again, Louisa slipped from the Green Room and returned to the back stairs. She raced across the landing, past the back entry and the guard standing with his back to the door, and over to the top of the cellar stairs.

A distinctive feminine voice made Louisa freeze. She lingered a moment, soft lamplight spilling along the lush hallway behind her. Yet, even as she stared at the dark, dank cellar steps, Louisa imagined the opulence and comfort of Ambassador Menabrea's lounge and the deadly woman who kept his company. Louisa shook off her discontent and managed the lower stairs as she had the attic ones until her feet met firm wood. No dirt floors for the rich.

Dark, hulking shapes loomed in the near-absolute black. Faint, filtered light from the porch sconces and street lamps trickled in through small, high windows.

This is it. If the Contessa had Morrie anywhere in this house, it would be the cellar — and that meant Bug or Scythe wasn't far off.

She couldn't risk sparking an orb, so Louisa used her other senses. She touched the all-cedar cabinets that held wilted files. She ran her fingers over long, sharp-scented pine tables, uneven kitchen chairs, and three-legged stools. Smooth, musty boxes stood in towers around the outer edge of the space, and wide paths **labyrinthed** through it all.

On the far side, the cool metal of a knob chilled her fingertips.

Louisa rested her ear against the door and held her breath.

Silence.

She turned the knob, gun raised, and sprinted right into a spiderweb. Louisa wiped the sticky strands from her face and hair, hoping whoever lived in it hadn't fallen onto her person.

A dense cold permeated the darkness and pressed against her body. She reached out. Jars of preserves lined tiered shelves that stretched across the front of the house.

No bad guys.

No Morrie.

An anguished cry threatened to overwhelm her. *He has to be here! I've missed something.*

Louisa backtracked through the basement, her eyes now fully adjusted to the lack of light. She let her fingertips dance from object to object as her gaze desperately searched through the black to something beyond.

Her heart ticked away vital minutes as she stood in the middle of the vast space, interloping in the Italian Embassy. If Hersh knew where she was, she'd be imprisoned for life. If the Ambassador or his men found her, she'd be held for international espionage and tortured.

Get out while you still can, her mother's voice echoed.

I can't leave him.

He's not here, Louanna.

Panic bubbled up from Louisa's stomach and flooded her every nerve, erasing rational thought. That suppressed scream pushed harder and harder against her chest.

And then she saw it.

One stack of boxes skewed slightly. Louisa's heart jumped. She hurried under the stairs and looked behind the cardboard tower at what should have been a solid cement-block wall. A thin bank of light glowed across the threshold of a hidden door. This one had a lock. Louisa crouched before the keyhole and peered into the secret room. She caught her breath.

Morrie.

He sat tied to a wooden chair, slumped, that damn electric net still over him. Louisa pulled every last bit of information about that device from Ryn—the more you struggled the stronger the zap. This wasn't the end. She clenched her teeth, anger overriding surprise and fear. *Those bloody bastards.*

She turned the knob, ready to burst in, shocked it wasn't actually locked. But that half-second of hesitation allowed Joe's voice purchase in her mind.

Wait.

She obeyed. He'd never steered her wrong, not even the night she'd had her pants handed to her in that barn brawl. Louisa inhaled slowly and looked through the keyhole again—around Morrie this time.

Always assess the situation before you enter a conversation or a room, her mother said. She'd intended the lesson for a more refined social environment, but it applied just as well here.

Okay. The light is on. The door is unlocked. The Contessa is upstairs. It's quiet. Bug and Scythe argue constantly. There's no arguing. Likely only one of the Judge's puppets is inside. Bug won't have his fire launcher in the embassy. Scythe might have her swords, but she'd be hard-pressed to use them in such tight quarters.

Louisa pulled one of the two surviving spheres from her pouch—the smokescreen.

Then Ryn had her say. *The Ambassador won't have the same kind of protection as my father, but what he does have will be lethal.*

Louisa hadn't detected a second perimeter guard, so probably only one watched outside, and the ambassador's bodyguard protected the inside. That meant if one of the thieves was on hostage duty, it would be the Contessa who relieved them for meals and ablutions. And there was no way of knowing how long ago that may have happened.

Bollocks.

Still, she had to smile. It was nice having more than one advisor in her head for a change. But Morrie's voice remained silent—both in her head and in the room before her.

Enough!

Louisa burst through the door. She swung her arm up to smash the orb. An elbow caught her in the side of the head. Bright sparks flashed in front of her eyes as she staggered into the room.

"How ..." escaped her lips.

"Don't you know it's polite to knock before entering a room?" Scythe cackled.

Of course, they'd have some kind of secret signal. *Damnit.* Between blinks, Louisa caught the deadly thief reaching for her knuckle blades tucked up in the knot of her ponytail. Louisa smashed the orb and sprang at the *halfinch*, catching her off guard. They fell against the packed earthen wall.

Scythe pushed Louisa off and kicked her in the chest. She stumbled across the narrow room into a long table. The water jug and glasses clattered. Louisa sucked in air past the pain compressing her lungs. She ran at Scythe again, keeping the thief on the defensive. Scythe swung a punch. Louisa ducked and jabbed her in the side, then *pas de Bourée'd* away and held her arms up, ready to fight. Louisa wasn't trained in the martial arts, but she was familiar with Scythe's favorite moves and the general rhythm of the cutpurse's style.

Louisa blocked a side kick with her arm bracer, the impact jarring but not bruise-worthy. Fists connected with flesh and feet met body parts. Always Louisa kept moving: circling, weaving, dancing in unexpected ways.

We don't have time, Morrie's voice invaded her thoughts. She glanced at his still form, lifelessly propped in the chair, incapacitated by the threat of electricity. As long as he remained still, it wouldn't shock him.

Scythe dove at Louisa, shoulder to stomach.

Louisa gasped and fell, the thief toppling with her.

Fight! Joe demanded.

She pulled her knees to her chest and rabbit-kicked Scythe. Louisa used the momentum to roll backward. Glass shattered as the *halfinch* landed on the table. Scythe scrambled up. Louisa smashed her last orb, blasting the thief back. She swung her leg out, taking down the cutpurse. Scythe's head hit the corner of the table and she collapsed.

A pang of horror exploded in Louisa's gut, but the woman lay there, still breathing. Louisa glanced from the broken glass to the thief to Morrie.

Hurry!

She grabbed the screwdriver from her coat pocket and wrapped the metal shaft with the bottom of her coat. *Wood is less likely to conduct electricity,* Ryn's voice echoed. Louisa had to get this right the first time. If she jostled the net, the movement would activate it again. She smashed the sturdy wooden handle into the net's control until it lay in pieces. With the chance of setting off the kinetic current disabled, she yanked the wires out of the box and tossed the whole thing off Morrie.

Louisa fell to her knees before him and lifted his pale, sweat-soaked face in her hands. Ryn said he'd be fine if he didn't move. If he tried to escape, the circuits would connect and he'd be shocked relative to the energy exerted on the wires. If he did this repeatedly it might kill him ...

"Morrie." She gasped. A large welt ballooned his cheek and purple bruises tracked along his jaw and around his eye. Sandy curls escaped around the edges of his hooded mask — they'd taken it off to identify him and shoved it back up again.

Why? To dehumanize him? To track him later? Blackmail?

He still didn't stir. Her chest ached, but not from the fight. This went deeper. She followed his arms back behind the chair to the rope strangling his wrists raw. He'd tried to loosen them. Her fingers wouldn't fit between the cinched threads. Louisa grabbed her screwdriver from the floor and used it to leverage the knots.

Come on. Come on!

Long, dark curls hung in Louisa's way, clinging to her moist brow as the binds loosened only marginally. She dropped the tool and dug her finger into the shallow hollows.

The distinctive slice of metal blades scissored the air. Louisa looked up as the dark beauty of the Contessa appeared over her razor fan in the doorway.

"I didn't think you'd give up so easily. Killing you now will save a lot of effort in the end." The Contessa narrowed her eyes.

Louisa stood slowly. She had not come here to die. Her hand hovered over her Blunderbuss, loaded with Ryn's new ammo. She almost wished the modified casings were lethal after all. Louisa took in the whole of the enemy before her. If the fight with Scythe had brought the Contessa, the ambassador's guards wouldn't be far behind.

Not good.

But the woman wore an evening gown, under which sat a corset and layers of fabric. The Contessa didn't engage — she waited for reinforcements.

"Run ..." Morrie whispered in her head, or was that out loud? He was always telling her to run.

Louisa charged the Contessa. She wasn't leaving without Morrie. The woman changed her stance and sliced the bladed fan to decapitate. Louisa knocked the Contessa's hand aside and ducked, spinning away from a dagger hidden behind the woman's skirts. Between Scythe and Morrie taking up space on the floor, room to maneuver grew scarce.

A well-aimed kick knocked the small blade from the Contessa's hand, but she refused to move away from the door. The woman gave a wicked grin and whipped the lethal fan at Louisa. The guardian twisted out of the way only to come face to face with the Contessa's gun — pointed straight at Louisa's head.

"This ends now," the woman said and growled.

Louisa snapped up the Blunderbuss.

Both women shot.

The Contessa fell back.

Louisa spun, pain igniting her body. She gasped.

"Run!" Morrie yelled.

Louisa glanced over her shoulder at the man who'd taken hold of her heart. She opened her mouth to protest, but his vivid eyes glistened silver in the low light as his stare pulsed past her. Louisa whirled around. Footsteps tromped down the stairs.

"Now! For God's sake go," he said, gasping from the effort.

She jumped over the downed Contessa and slipped into the dark under the stairs as a near-identical guard to the one outside barreled into view, revolver raised.

Louisa burst from the shadows, forcing his arms up. Pain sliced through her. The gun fired. He stumbled. Louisa raced around him, up the stairs, and burst out the back door straight into the other guard. She hit him like a cannonball, falling with him but rolling out of the tumble and back up onto her feet. She dashed off into the night, leaving a faint trail of blood in her wake.

Chapter IV

The Final Countdown

Louisa peeled back the gauze from her upper shoulder as she stared at herself in the vanity mirror and watched the skin pucker and twist. When she got home last night, she'd torn a hastily devised bandage off, torturing herself with the physical ache as punishment for failing Morrie. The fresh gauze went on without salve and now stuck.

She uncapped her mother's old perfume bottle — filled with spirits — and splashed a portion of the contents on her raw wound. Louisa grimaced, her features distorting with pain, before wiping the excess from her arm and daubing the bullet wound. A graze only, but it hurt like the devil. The dram of honey she'd stolen from the kitchen would be tacky enough to hold new dressings in place.

The doorknob rattled.

Louisa jumped.

"Hey, Lou, the door's locked. Are you all right? We need to leave soon and you haven't eaten yet," Elenore called.

"I'm fine. I'm just finishing up." Louisa wrapped fresh gauze around her upper arm. The dark pink scars on her forearms taunted her. Last time, Morrie had patched her up—just like the first time. He was supposed to be home, not trapped in a hidden cellar at the Italian Embassy.

"I must have bumped the latch by mistake. I've got my hands tangled in my hair. I can't open the door right now." The lie panged her morals. Louisa slipped on a light gray chemise, her breath catching at the jolt of pain from her arm. Gingerly, she pulled on a charcoal gray vest over her corset before attacking her unruly mass of curls.

"Can you bring my gloves down with you? It's chillier than I expected, and these light ones won't do."

Louisa glanced around. "Where are they?"

"My bedside table. Top drawer. Thank you!"

"You're welcome. I'll be right down." Louisa

rolled two French braids around each other and pinned them into a tight bun on the back of her head. Every twist and weave sliced daggers along her wounded arm. She ground her teeth and worked through the ache.

Louisa stood, leaned forward, and studied the dark hollows under her eyes. She grabbed Elenore's concealer and daubed some on before retrieving the gloves and unlocking the bedroom door. She nearly collided with her roommate. Louisa gasped and held a hand to her heart. Elenore did the same, shakily laughing it off. Louisa handed the other woman the gloves, and they hurried down the stairs.

Bennett stood by the door, holding Louisa's frock for her. She bit the inside of her cheek, raised both arms, and shrugged into the coat with his help.

"Aren't you going to eat something?" Elenore asked.

"Did *you* eat?" Louisa countered.

Elenore blushed.

"Didn't think so. We can feast after the presentation."

Bennett shook his head at them. "Are we ready then? Mrs. Abernathy's landau is waiting." He picked up his satchel, and Louisa collected hers.

"I'll meet up with you." She tried to keep her voice from shaking.

"What's that now?" Bennett crossed his arms, a stern set to his features.

"Mr. Tweed asked if I could help him set up his equipment. He's bringing a few extra items to make sure he documents everything perfectly — asked for my help. You were going to have the pilots work with you loading their nets, right?"

"Yes, but —"

"I won't be long. I'll still be there for the second check, well before launch." She thought of giving a reassuring smile, but her face wouldn't cooperate. Instead, Louisa headed for the door, waving the others to follow.

"But what about Elly?" Bennett asked, close on Louisa's heels.

Louisa turned and held Bennett's hand with both of hers, a bold gesture, but one no different than any blood sibling might make. "I can count on you to be a gentleman on the drive over, can't I? Do

I need to say something to Arthur? If I do, Mrs. Abernathy's driver is likely to tell her I needed to say something and then—"

"No. No, that's quite all right. You go help Morrie. Elly and I can manage just fine until you arrive." He slipped from her hands, opened the carriage door, and helped Elenore in. They pointedly avoided looking at each other. Had it been any other day, Louisa would've laughed and let the merriment ease her nerves. As it was, she barely managed a small smile before waving them off and rushing to catch the train. She'd already let Morrie down. She couldn't do that to Bennet too.

* * *

Louisa stared at Morrie's front door, turning the back door key over and over again in her coat pocket. She'd forgotten to replace it the night she'd apologized for kissing him—his gruff behavior had set her on edge, and the key had remained in her Phoenix duster until this morning. A brisk wind bit her exposed cheeks and ears.

She couldn't risk jumping over the garden wall in broad daylight, nor could she be seen trying to gain entrance to a salon before mid-day. Besides,

Joe wouldn't be in yet. If Louisa wanted to get her hands on Morrie's equipment, that meant going in the front door.

But she didn't live there. If her hunch didn't pan out and someone caught her, the constabulary wouldn't be far behind.

What if he escaped on his own? I did disable the net. No one but Ryn could fix it. Hope surged in Louisa's chest, compelling her to walk up and knock on the door.

No one answered.

That means nothing. He lives downstairs. He could be there or washing up or any number of things. The image of his inflamed cheek and the multiple bruises swelling his face turned her stomach. She waited the requisite length of time before a civilized person should knock again, but every second ate at her insides.

After ten minutes total waiting time, Louisa had to concede the Contessa still had him. *Or maybe not. Maybe he's asleep. Between the torture and threat of a zapping from Ryn's net, he's probably exhausted.*

Louisa plucked the key from her pocket and jammed it into the lock. It wouldn't turn. Terror burned cold, then hot, through her body.

No. It has to work. It has to. I'm not wrong.

She shook the key and tried again.

Yes!

She yanked it back out and entered the house. Dust motes hung in the air. It took a moment to orient herself—she was used to entering through the back door. But that was the proverbial key.

The blind alley. The garden wall. The side entrance that likely used to be for the servants and now catered to that clientele. The backdoor likely never had a key access, only a deadbolt. When Morrie decided to open his home as their headquarters, it would have made sense to request a locksmith to fashion a new lock for the old key. No sense in having to keep track of three when he didn't even use one of them.

Louisa got her bearings and headed for the back stairs down to the tavern.

"Morrie! Morrie, I'm here. Are you okay? Morrie!"

But the door on the lower landing revealed only an empty bar, and an even emptier cot in the small room at the end of the hall. Louisa clung to the stair railing, her legs ready to give way.

He's not here. They still have him.

A sob slipped past her lips. Still clinging to the railing, she laid her head on the back of her hands. Her sore arm complained, but she didn't care.

I couldn't have done this without you, Lou, Bennett's words echoed from the past weeks. Louisa knew it wasn't true—she just helped speed things along. But he was counting on her. This presentation would make or break him in the eyes of his peers and his betters. The Queen needed a solution to the drought. Elenore stood to make a proper name for herself ...

Louisa sucked in a shaky breath and forced herself to stand tall. They needed her. She couldn't do anything for Morrie now except not interfere as Shadow Phoenix — but that didn't mean she could give up on everyone else.

Louisa ran back up to the main floor and into the dining room. The faces of the thieves posted on the wall followed her every move as she skirted the planning table and collected his photography equipment. She made three trips to the front door with satchels and boxes with handles. Louisa didn't know what should be brought or left behind, so she collected it all and hailed a Steamie. Her arm burned the entire time — penance for her crimes.

Chapter V

A Shadow of Jaguars

As Louisa did her best to set up Morrie's photography equipment, more and more guests arrived. She looked up from the notes in his journal, which she'd found in a worn leather satchel on the drive over. The Sky Port officials worked with the constabulary to set up a checkpoint. Only those with invitations could enter the small amphitheater set up below the Sky Walk on the west side, near the closest lift.

Inspector Hersh stood talking with a pair of gentlemen from the Society of Engineers as they all observed Bennett and Elenore working with the pilots to fill the dispersal nets. The six Minis moored to the ground, not more than a stone's throw away, would make for a grand picture — but Louisa had no idea how to work the device. She

didn't even know if she'd attached the right lens —
there were three of varying lengths and even a
hand-held version that looked ... experimental.

Her frustration rose. Hersh had ignored her
midnight advice to beef up the watch in
anticipation of another hit. She'd told him Phoenix
would be "indisposed." She should be helping load
the orbs, not learning how to operate this stuff.
What she needed was a stand-in. Louisa could help
Morrie with the write-up after the thieves let him
go. She just had to find someone else to take the
pictures.

Louisa stared out over the increasing masses.
Dark blue uniforms dotted the multicolored
tailorings of the crowd, but still not enough to
handle what the Judge had in store for today. She
sighed and focused on the task at hand.

*What I need is someone who's good with machinery.
An ... engineer.* Louisa gave herself a mental slap.
The stands were full of them. She knew the name of
every person in attendance, and their profession —
she just didn't know what they looked like.
However, she did know what seat number they
were assigned!

Louisa abandoned the equipment and headed for the stands. Few guests were seated yet. She glanced at the glassed-in central fourth tier, still unoccupied. Methodically, Louisa ran through the names in alphabetical order in her head, as they'd been listed by Bennett on the forms.

As she searched the bustling and chatty crowd, Louisa's heart hammered in her chest. Of the first three names on the list who were mechanical engineers, only one sat with his wife — and he was so frail and withered Louisa couldn't ask him for help.

Come on. Come on. I need to be with Bennett and Elly ...

She scanned the risers for the next potential photographer, but her gaze kept returning to Morrie's empty seat. Except, this time, it wasn't empty. Her stomach jumped. *Not Morrie.* A page-boy with a small notebook sat scribbling. Hot anger shot through her veins. *What's he doing there? He's not on the list.* Louisa stepped toward the imposter.

"Miss. Wicker?"

She halted and turned. "Mr. Green." Louisa took in his companion. "Mr. Digsby. G-glad you could both make it."

"Perfect day, isn't it?" Mr. Green, the environmental scientist who worked at the Royal Botanical Garden, asked.

She hadn't even noticed the day. Louisa looked up. Light gray, fast-moving stratocumulus clouds in the lower atmosphere held promise. They extended all the way east into their target zone — to seed as they traveled closer to the small semi-circle of spectators and representatives.

A sudden flash caught Louisa's eye. She didn't look away from her conversants—that would be rude—but her breathing quickened. *Calm down. It's likely just the other newspapers taking advantage of the dispersal orb loading shot.*

"Yes, the skies are filled with potential. Dear gentlemen, have you seen Miss. Chalmers by chance? I was hoping to make her acquaintance before the launch."

The Minister for Agriculture, Mr. Digsby, smiled broadly. "Indeed, my dear. She's just come through the gate. She's the redhead standing with—"

An explosion quaked the ground and punched

the air. Everyone dropped, yelling—everyone except Louisa. She spun toward the wild volley of flames engulfing Elenore's airship.

Bug! You little bastard.

Louisa shot toward the billowing flames, weaving through the assembled guests, most of whom still crouched. The glass box remained empty. *Small miracles.* If the Queen went anywhere, she was fashionably late.

Firefighters tore out of the surrounding buildings. Alarms blared, black smoke filled the sky, and two pumper trucks pulled in close to the source of the flames. Police dressed in their blues converged with dozens of other men in civilian attire who comported themselves strangely like off-duty officers. Another small miracle—Hersh had actually listened to her. They were everywhere, like reversed shadows to the darker patrolmen.

Louisa raced toward Bennett, who held Elenore behind a wall of police and Sky Port officials. Louisa tried to navigate around the blockade to help the pilots, but a steel grip clamped over her arm and stopped her short.

She cried out and grabbed her sore shoulder as

she pivoted around to face her captor. "Inspector Hersh!"

He frowned.

"Louisa Wicker. Mr. Bennett's assistant. Please let me go. I need to help the pilots move their—"

"The authorities have it under control." He narrowed his eyes at her as if seeing her true intentions: finding the maniac who did this before he got away.

Wait, he can't think I'm involved?

Louisa jolted. Great blasts of water sizzled against the nearby flames. She looked around, frantic, taking everything in. He was right. The port authorities had hitched the low-moored Minis to transit vehicles and shuttled them away from the inferno. She inhaled a great breath and sighed, relaxing in the inspector's grasp. He let go.

"You're the one who can smell the difference between scorched accelerants," he said, and walked forward, making her shuffle backward toward Bennett and Elenore.

"Yes." *He remembers that? He believed me? I was so sure he thought me an imbecile.* Louisa turned and embraced Elenore just as two plain-clothed officers dragged forward a struggling midget.

It's him! He did it, she wanted to cry as Bug defended his innocence and denied all accusations.

"Inspector, he was caught fleeing the scene," one officer said.

"That's not a crime. I was scared. I'm afraid of fire."

It took every ounce of self-control not to condemn the small man and blow her cover.

"Should we let him go?" the officer asked.

Hersh looked ready to believe the desperate *halfinch.*

"No!" Louisa cried, drawing all eyes to her. *What can I say?* "He's not on the guest list."

"I work here," Bug said pulling his arm free of the officer and rubbing it.

She knew he didn't, but by the time they could find someone to verify his claim, he'd have escaped.

Do something. He can't get away with this. "He—"

"He's the arson!" The claim saved her from revealing herself.

Louisa's heart launched into her throat. A

battered and bruised but very much alive Morrie pushed through the crowd in crisp, clean gear and a low-slung cap, waving the hand-held camera she'd brought. Louisa stared at him openmouthed.

"I have proof. I got it on film." He panted, trying to catch his breath.

Hersh made a motion with his hand, and both officers gripped Bug's arms.

"And who are you?" Hersh asked.

"He's my documenter, Morrison Tweed," Bennett provided, discreetly eyeing the man's condition below the brim of his cap.

"That's right. I was taking pictures of the aircraft and the loading procedures when I caught that man using some kind of flame launcher on the lead ship. I snapped a shot and hollered at him, but he took off. It's fortunate you have so many men here today, Inspector, or he might have escaped."

Louisa's heart swelled. Even a mess, even as he claimed a victory for good, he still managed to find a way to rub Hersh's nose in the fact that Shadow Phoenix was one of the good guys. Not that Morrie knew she'd confronted Hersh, but it had that effect all the same.

"You have a picture of this man committing the crime?" Hersh took Morrie aside and gave the signal for his men to follow.

Louisa moved to join them but stopped at Elenore's aching sob. Torn, Louisa turned to embrace her friend once more.

"It's over," Elenore cried.

Bennett looked at the ground, forlorn, before staring up at the wet, metal husk of the lead airship.

"It's not." Louisa held Elenore out at arm's length and then punched Bennett in the shoulder.

"Ow. What's that for? She's right. We calculated six ships—"

"So what?" Louisa looped an arm through each of theirs and turned them to face the remaining five Minis now at a safe distance from the wreckage. "We divide the extra orbs evenly between the remaining ships, and Elly sails with Captain Maddox, her Second." Both of them faced her, brightening.

"Of course!" cried Bennett, dancing them around.

"I can't sail with him alone," Elenore worried.

Bennett stopped his wild caper. "Lou can ride

with you."

Louisa's stomach dropped. A fanfare of trumpets blasted the air, and the three turned for the official presentation of the Queen.

Chapter VI

The Amazing & Truly Incredible Vaulting Stomach

Every time Louisa tried to connect with Morrie, someone needed her. Most especially Bennett, who completely forgot his childhood etiquette lessons. Louisa needed to provide an immediate tutorial before he could think of addressing the Queen and all those assembled.

Louisa also had to oversee the dividing of the additional dispersal orbs among the remaining ships and reassure the Sky Port authorities that Bennett's spheres were not the cause of the fire — they just happened to give it a hell of an extra kick. Now, as she hurried over to the area where she'd set up Morrie's equipment, Captain Maddox's voice rose above the hum of the waiting crowd and the airships' engines.

"Absolutely not. Give me your notes and I'll lead the Minis. That's the purpose of a Second. So let me do my job."

Louisa couldn't hear Elenore's response, but based on her low tone, slumped shoulders, and bowed head, he'd cowed her out of her earlier confidence. Louisa searched for Morrie but didn't see him nearby—he also had a job to do, though Louisa still couldn't believe he'd escaped. She walked up beside Elenore mid-stutter.

"-s-see how important it is f-for me to be in the air."

Louisa stood close enough that their shoulders touched. Elenore didn't look at her, but she stood a little taller.

"Is there a problem, Captain?" Louisa addressed Maddox.

"Not at all. I was just explaining to Captain Rathburn how efficient it would be if there weren't three of us vying for room in the Mini, and if she gave me her notes, I could lead the aerial presentation for her."

"Ah, yes, an excellent suggestion."

Elenore stared at Louisa, aghast.

"Except Mr. Bennett hired Captain Rathburn to lead, and since you're her Second, she has every right to commandeer your vessel to ensure the job is completed to his specifications. If you're concerned the three of us will bump elbows, we can arrange for her to fly solo. How does that sound?"

It sounded brilliant to Louisa. One less trip up into the heavens.

His eyes widened.

"Captain Maddox," Elenore's voice rose confident and clear. "As I was saying, I do believe the best course of action is for all of us to travel together so we can complete the jobs assigned to us. Don't you agree?"

He gave a curt nod.

"Miss. Wicker and I will board shortly. Mr. Bennett would like a word with us before we depart."

"Certainly, Captain. I await your next instructions." He gave her a sharp salute and went to complete the final pre-boarding inspection of his aircraft.

Elenore watched Maddox saunter out of sight and collapsed into Louisa's arms.

"Oh, dear Lord, Lou. If you hadn't arrived, I would've given up and agreed."

Louisa hugged her friend and held Elenore's chin, though it pained her arm to do so. "Why didn't you just tell him what I did? It's the truth. He knows it. He signed the contract."

"I just lost my ship. I know what that feels like, and I didn't want to inflict that on anyone else."

Louisa gave a grim smile and nodded. "You're a good person, Elly." She gave Elenore's shoulder a gentle squeeze.

"There you two are."

Louisa and Elenore turned to face Bennett.

"How does it look?" he asked, glancing from one young lady to the other.

"All set," they replied together and smiled.

"How are *you* doing?" Louisa asked, staring past him to the crowd gathered on the risers and the Queen on display in her glass box.

"Everyone came. I can't believe it. We have over two hundred people here to witness history in the making. I've been going over your pointers."

He put his hands in his pockets, took them out again, crossed and uncrossed his arms. Finally, he checked his watch. "Oh my, it's time." He looked high and low and turned nearly all-ways 'round and back again.

Louisa tugged Elenore's elbow, and both women engulfed Bennett in a hug. He did his best to hug them back, chuckling.

"You'll do brilliant, Andrew," Elenore said.

"You've got this. Deep breaths now, just like we practiced." Louisa rotated him around and pointed him to the speaking trumpet set in the middle of the semicircle of guests.

Bennett strode into his future.

Louisa gingerly grasped Elenore's elbow and turned her to face the opposite direction. "Captain Rathburn, I do believe we have a job to do."

Elenore gave a nervous laugh and hurried with Louisa across the lawn to the new staging area for the fleet of Minis. Luckily for Louisa, they'd be taking off from the ground instead of from the Sky Port above.

As she boarded Captain Maddox's Mini, Louisa glanced out behind her one last time and finally caught sight of Morrie. Her stomach flipped. He'd repositioned his tripod closer to the main event and stood with his back to her, fulfilling his promise to Bennett. A flush crept over Louisa, her body warming as joy burst inside her.

He's safe.

She hadn't failed him entirely.

"Come on, Louisa. We're getting the green flag," Elenore called from inside the gondola.

Louisa ducked in through the side access hatch and levered it up behind her. Maddox double checked that it was secure and signaled the ground crew to release the moorings.

Elenore sat, out of the way, on a raised chair at the back, the roof above pulled open to allow her first-hand access to wind readings and an unobstructed view of the sky. She wrapped her scarf tighter about her neck and pulled a pair of flight goggles over her eyes. In her gloved hands, she held a pair of brass flight instruments, used to help her determine where best, and at which altitude, to direct the fleet to disperse their orbs. Louisa wasn't familiar with the finer calculations necessary, but no trace of fear or concern marred her friend's features — she was in her element.

"Sit there." Maddox pointed to a hinged piece of wood in the middle of the port-side hull.

Louisa pulled it down. Two legs dropped to steady the front of the seat and she sat. Hers would be the easy job this time. She watched the pair of them work independently of one another and yet toward a common goal. Maddox used his wheeled stool to full advantage, giving Louisa a sense of what it must be like when Elenore's brother piloted his Mini in the races.

Outside the side portholes, the colorful oblong balloons of the other ships rose around them. Maddox had an impressive view through a sweeping bank of windows across the bow of the ship. Louisa slipped off her frock coat and set it on a nearby peg. Even with the hatch open, the engines produced a fair bit of heat.

The bustling Sky Port burst into view as they rose higher, and dozens of travelers waved from the moving walkway and many of the platforms. It was a city in the sky, with intricate networks and full-sized airships set to voyage across England, Europe, and even to the Americas. Louisa could appreciate the majesty of it, so long as she didn't have to stand on it.

They rose higher and faster into the clouds. Above the Sky Port, Maddox fell into a comfortable routine as he cranked the flanking directional propellers from a pair of devices inside the cockpit.

The blue Mini rose out beyond the starboard portholes, majestic against the paler blue and white surrounding them. The green Mini rose port side and the other two pulled into formation aft. But the sky blurred below the blue Mini. A twinge in Louisa's constitution compelled her off the hinged seat and across to the window.

She peered outside and gasped. Hundreds of dispersal orbs prematurely littered the sky! *But why? What happened? Are the nets faulty? We triple-checked everything …*

And then she saw it.

A flash of red spidering along the outer rigging of the not-so-distant ship as it kept strict formation. A glint of steel and the rest of blue's payload dispersed.

"Louisa!" Elenore shouted.

"I see it!" Louisa bolted to the rope ladder to

stand near Elenore, who gazed out across the upper deck.

"What's going on?" Maddox yelled.

Louisa clung to the ladder, trying to see outside. "A stowaway is sabotaging the blue Mini's dispersal nets. The orbs are deploying too soon." She looked everywhere for that stain of red. "Elly, do you see her?"

"Her who?" The young pilot twisted around, but not fast enough.

"Me." An all-too-familiar cackle rent the air as Scythe's fist connected with Elenore's head. The pilot slumped and lost purchase of her chair. Louisa grabbed Elenore around the waist, ducking a boot aimed at her head. The pair dropped to the floor inside the Mini as Scythe swung in through the opening, wearing some kind of folded contraption on her back.

Louisa yanked an incoherent Elenore out of the cutpurse's warpath.

"Maddox! Behind you," Louisa called.

He twisted about, startled to see the lithe Filipino aboard his ship.

"What in blazes? Who the hell are you?"

"Your worst nightmare." Scythe attacked, catching him off guard.

Louisa leaned Elenore against the wall, the young woman's groans reassuring her that Elenore remained conscious but stunned.

Maddox thrust his fists out, boxing the air instead of the thief. Scythe's quick footwork and flexible body kept one step ahead of the broad Captain. Louisa tried to find an opening, a way to join the fray, but before she could, Scythe kicked Maddox in the delicates and brought him to his knees. She then whipped around and kicked him alongside the head.

He collapsed.

Louisa dropped to her knees and clasped her hands in prayer.

Scythe laughed and turned her back on Louisa, heading to release catches for their nets.

But Louisa wasn't praying. God had never done her any favors—he helped those who helped themselves. She sprang from her knees to her feet and tackled the thief.

Louisa wrapped her legs around the thin woman's waist and her arm about the cutpurse's neck. The strange contraption on the thief's back dug into Louisa's body, and kept her from getting a solid grip. Scythe gasped and jabbed Louisa in the ribs. Her grasp loosened. Scythe twisted and smashed Louisa into the wall. Louisa let go. Dropping to her knees, she sucked in air, desperate to fill her lungs.

Scythe caught her balance and kicked. Louisa grabbed the thief's foot and twisted along with the force, yanking the blighter off her feet. She hit the deck, hard, but rolled away from Louisa's stomp, reaching for the knot of a bun at the base of her ponytail.

"I don't think so." Louisa grabbed Maddox's stool and smashed it at the thief.

Scythe blocked the blow with her arm but didn't get to her twin talon-blades. The woman narrowed her eyes at Louisa.

"I know you."

"I doubt that."

Scythe cracked a sly grin. "Phoenix, my dear. How lovely to *see* you."

"Can't say the same about you, Scythe."

"I should've known you wouldn't listen."

The two women circled the confined space. Elenore stirred.

"Doesn't matter. My partner's safe and I have a job to do—disguise or no. This ends now." Louisa never broke eye contact. "Elly, no one's driving this thing. Keep us on course."

Elenore groaned and scrambled to the helm.

Scythe attacked.

A flurry of kicks and hits buffeted Louisa from all sides. She blocked and ducked what she could but landed hard as Scythe took out her feet. Louisa braced for a cutting blow, but it never came.

Scythe scrambled up the ladder to the open deck above. Time whirled as the airships drew closer to their mark. Louisa raced topside after the thief, who ran right off the port-side of the deck into the air. Twin kite-sails snapped open from the compact contraption on her back, and she glided across to the green Mini toward an unsuspecting pilot. Scythe hadn't run away—she'd opted for an easier target.

"Dammit!" Louisa dropped to her knees and yelled into the gondola. "Get me as close to the green Mini as possible. Now!"

Louisa stood, but the sudden directional change of the engines sent her sprawling. She clung to the rigging and stumbled against the buffeting wind toward the edge of the ship. Her stomach lurched. Bile rose in her throat, but she swallowed it back.

I can do this.

The world was so far below she couldn't make out any distinct shapes. She had to get over to that Mini and stop Scythe or the presentation would be ruined — along with Bennett's and Elenore's reputations.

Louisa stared at the green balloon of the airship getting closer and rising higher. Elenore had little room to spare. Louisa scanned the deck.

I don't know what to do!

Shut up and think, already.

She grabbed a loose bit of rigging and pulled the lower knot of the line free as Scythe disappeared into the cockpit.

No!

Louisa shook out the long rope, turned, and vaulted off the side of the airship.

Chapter VII
Featherless

Icy wind slashed through Louisa's wool suit. Tears stung her eyes. She squinted at the looming deck of the green blimp as her knuckles whitened in a death-grip on the rope. She wrapped a leg in the lower line to keep from sliding down. The length of rope from Maddox's rigging arced up, slowing toward the apex. Louisa didn't want to let go, but she had to.

She screamed. Throat burning, Louisa popped her grip and flung her arms wide. She plummeted toward the deck two stories below and slammed into it. The angle of descent forcing her into a stomach-skid.

Louisa choked and spat blood. Gasping, she pushed up onto her hands and vomited. The bile from her empty stomach seared her already raw throat. Her arms shook trying to hold her up. She wanted desperately to curl into a ball and cry, but that would be giving up on the people she cared about most.

She took in several short, halting breaths and pushed herself into a crouch.

Scythe, grumbling to herself about seized cranks being more trouble than they're worth, gained the upper deck and pulled a talon free from her hair. She narrowed her eyes at Louisa and shifted her stance from casual to deadly.

"I won't let you do this," Louisa yelled, standing. She shook from the cutting wind, the height, and her insane leap. But her voice belied a strength she didn't feel. It grounded her.

Scythe glanced at the netting clamps on the port side. She dove for them instead of Louisa.

"No!" Louisa scrambled after the *halfinch* with a jolt of energy she didn't know she possessed.

Scythe slashed at the ties, but her small blade only bit into the hefty netting. The cords remained intact, for now. Louisa dove at the thief's legs, knocking her over. Scythe kicked Louisa off and rolled aside, jumping to her feet again. Louisa followed, ducking a vicious slice as Scythe reached for the twin blade.

Cold condensation dewed Louisa's face and neck as the ship entered the largest cloud. Wisps of vapor clung like fog to the rigging, obscuring the wide sky.

A grinding snap drew both fighters' attention as the net's clamps released. The lead lines slipped effortlessly through the cinching rings. Hundreds of orbs filled the air.

Oh, I hope it's enough …

Bug had taken them from six ships to five, and Scythe's culling had brought them down to four. They'd made it rain with far less before, but those were paltry showers that soaked people, not the ground. Bennet needed a downpour of drenching rain to convince the Society of Engineers, and the Queen, that his design worked. The Judge's lackeys had certainly done damage this time.

A sly smile split Scythe's menacing stare. "And now, I get to finish you off."

Louisa had no lightning orbs, punch orbs, or smokescreen. Her steel pipe lay somewhere on the

Italian Embassy grounds, and her Blunderbuss remained wrapped in her Shadow Phoenix disguise at the bottom of her satchel tucked in the far corner of Bennett's workshop. In broad daylight this night bird stood featherless — or nearly.

Scythe whipped her talon-blades through the air. Louisa ducked and dodged the barrage, bringing her arm up to block a malicious slice.

Metal clanged metal.

The talon blade bounced off Louisa's protected forearm.

Louisa took advantage of Scythe's momentary surprise and kicked her. The thief stumbled back. Louisa went on the offensive, channeling Joe's rhythms and music of the slaves to give her the strength she needed to endure.

Blow for blow, Louisa and Scythe circuited the frosty air, sweat crystalizing on lashes and damp tendrils of hair. The two fighters battled as more and more orbs burst in the charged air around them, igniting the sky.

The green Mini rose out of the drop zone, following the sequence for the return run. Maddox's ship came level with the deck of the green Mini, quickly dropping away as hers climbed.

Scythe's foot slipped on the slick deck. She rotated into the fall, snapped open her shoulder-kite wings, and pushed off the edge of the deck.

Codswallop! I can't let her get away. Not again.

Louisa ran and launched herself into the air. She grabbed onto Scythe's legs and dragged her down. They crashed into Maddox's ship, tumbling over each other across the narrow deck. Louisa tucked her feet in and kicked the thief solidly in the chest. Scythe soared into the air, broken kite contraption flailing. She bounced once and disappeared over the side.

Louisa scrambled across the decking and peered over the edge, heart in her throat. *Did I kill her?* Her teeth chattered. Her arms and hands shook.

The netting-stays reeled back into place, finalizing the dispersal orb drop. The clamps clicked shut. And there, in the bottom of the net, writhed a long, lean, red body surrounded by broken kite arms and rumpled material.

Louisa's insides lurched and jumped. She

swallowed several times, taking deep breaths, but they refused to settle. Louisa pulled herself up on the rigging and searched for a length of rope. With frozen hands, she wove the opening at the top where the net met the hull, tying it off the best she could.

Scythe stopped flailing and curled into herself against the cold, using the kite fabric as a shield. Louisa stumbled toward the open hatch and dropped into the descending Mini.

"Louisa!" Elenore cried, looking over her shoulder from the helm. Maddox rested unconscious, propped against the wall where Scythe had leveled him.

Her breath no longer frost-laden, Louisa embraced the warmth of the cabin. She crawled toward the starboard engine block, curled up like a dog, and collapsed.

* * *

"—uisa ..."

Huh?

"Louisa, can you hear me? We've docked. Oh, I'll have to fetch a physician."

"No." Louisa grabbed Elenore's arm before she

could stand, her hand icy against the pilot's warm skin.

"You're frozen. You need help."

The haze shrouding Louisa's brain lifted a little more. "No, I don't. I'm fine. I'll be fine." She grimaced as she sat up and got her bearings. Sore ribs and bruised forearms were a hell of a lot better than the way some of her battles had ended.

Scythe.

Louisa pulled Elenore to her feet. "Elly, the saboteur is trapped in the starboard net. She'll need a doctor and a police escort."

Elenore nodded, a wary look crossing her face. She turned, stiffly, to open the gangway hatch. Louisa followed her.

"Please, don't say anything about my involvement. If the Inspector finds out—if he puts the pieces together—"

"You know I can't lie, Lou," she whispered.

"Then just tell them you didn't see what happened. That's the truth, right? You saw me follow her out onto the top deck and then you focused on flying."

Elenore sighed and helped Louisa on with her

coat. Louisa glanced at Maddox, still unconscious.

"You'd better hurry. That woman outside needs immediate attention and the Captain isn't doing so well either. The stowaway hit his head in the fight and he might have a concussion."

"What about you? Aren't you coming too?"

"I'm going to keep an eye on the saboteur. We can't let her get away."

Elenore climbed out the side entry and the two women hurried onto their designated Sky Port platform. Louisa turned to head around the opposite side of the airship, pulling on her gloves, but a tug on her sleeve stopped her.

Elenore leaned close as the other pilots converged toward them. "Is it really true?" she whispered.

For a moment Louisa wasn't sure what she meant. Then Scythe's pronouncement rang through her ears *Phoenix, my dear. How lovely to see you.*

She could deny it outright, but if Elenore had heard the comment, she'd heard Louisa's response too.

"Plausible deniability, Elly. I won't confirm or deny it. Just, please, don't say anything or the next time you'll see me is behind bars."

The young pilot nodded and backed away. "We need a physician! A doctor! Someone!" The other pilots took up the call and the five of them dispersed, Elly heading down the lift to notify the ground crew and the constabulary.

Louisa snuck to the other side of the Mini's gondola and came face to face with Scythe. The thief snarled, still caught up in the netting where the orbs had been. Other than that, she didn't move. At least she was conscious.

Neither woman said a word. They just stared. After two long months, their rivalry came down to this. So much hate. So much destruction ...

Whistles blew.

Feet stomped.

The cavalry arrived—and Louisa disappeared. She slipped around the back of a small supply hut. Elenore led the charge back to Maddox's ship. Louisa blended in with the regular traffic on the elevated moving walkway, except she was the only one with a rigid stance and two hands sliding along the brass rail.

She staggered into the closest lift and clutched

the iron bars. The porter gave her an odd look that lingered a little too long about her face. An escaped tendril of hair fell across her nose. Louisa pushed it back behind her ear, but it popped free again. She groaned inwardly. Her misadventures had torn her hair loose from its braided bun. She probably looked like Medusa.

Anchoring her feet flat to the floor, she pushed her lower back against the decorative rail, removed her gloves, and quickly undid her hair. At the bottom, just before the door opened, she spun the mass of it into an untidy bun and jammed as many pins in it from her original hairstyle as possible to keep it in place. Fine stray hairs still tickled her forehead and cheeks, but the porter nodded his approval. She nodded back and exited, stashing the remaining pins into her coat pocket. Louisa maneuvered off the lift, legs threatening to fail, and walked right into a solid mass of tweed.

She looked up to apologize. Her knees gave out, but not before she threw her arms around Morrie. Louisa held him tight, burying her face into his neck and shoulder. His arms encircled her. He lifted her up just enough that she needn't worry about the use of her legs and tucked the two of them into an alcove next to a bank of offices in the lower station house.

Louisa trembled from head to foot. She met Morrie's gaze with a dozen questions, but one look into his calm gray eyes and she put her mouth to better use.

He met her kiss, firm but gentle. Louisa gave over to everything bubbling inside. Rules be damned, warnings be damned, and propriety be doubly damned.

She pulled back a little to catch her breath, then stiffened, realization dawning.

"Oh, no, I'm sorry."

Morrie chuckled. "For what? Certainly not for saving my life last night?"

"I did what now? You mean it worked? Deactivating the net—"

"That and the present you left behind were most helpful."

"Present? My screwdriver!"

"Yes. It came in very handy."

"I was so worried …" She caressed his bruised jaw up along the side of his face, tipping his cap back to expose the full effects of his time with the Contessa. Her breath hitched. He kissed her again, wiping away the thought that she should have done more—that she shouldn't have kissed him in the first place.

"Now, am I supposed to apologize? Is that the newest fad?" He smiled and she nearly melted.

"No, well, not really. I just—oh, I'm sorry for how I must taste." She hadn't had time to rinse her mouth after reacting poorly during her harrowing adventure.

Morrie chuckled again, deep and throaty. The rich resonance traveled from the base of her ear, through her chest, to her stomach, re-awakening the butterflies.

"You taste just fine." He caught her lips a third time. A fire ignited in her core, chasing away the last of the cold and the fear. She drank him in—at least until a crowd burst from the nearby lift.

Louisa and Morrie turned as one in their little hiding nook and watched Hersh parade a handcuffed Scythe before him. Two other officers flanked the pair, and Bennett and Elenore brought up the rear with a very much mobile Captain Maddox.

"Well, now, I get the feeling you had something to with all this?" Morrie's warm breath played with the loose curls against her forehead.

"You could say that. Phoenix might have shown up in civilian garb today — taking a feather from Hersh's cap with all the plain-clothes officers around. I'll not get the collar for this one though. I'll paint Maddox as the hero for standing up to Scythe, even though she knocked him out cold."

"And how did you catch her, way up there?"

"Would that be Hawk or Reporter Tweed asking?"

"Both of us are dying to find out. You'll have to fill me in on the details later. Right now" — he took her hand and led her from the alcove — "we'd best keep up. Mr. Bennett has a final speech yet to give and we both have our own duties to attend to." He slipped her hand into the crook of his arm, and they followed the parade out of the building.

The sky had grown marginally darker, but there was still no rain. It had never taken this long before. Louisa looked heavenward, searching for some sign that it hadn't all been in vain — that the Judge wouldn't win this round, for it could very well mean the end of the war if that were the case.

Hersh locked Scythe in a paddy wagon and personally rode back to the station with her. He'd sent Bug along before they'd taken to the sky.

Morrie stopped near the edge of the presentation semi-circle and set up the larger camera for the finale. The page boy who'd sat in Morrie's assigned seat in the stands came running up with the smaller hand-held camera slung around his neck.

"I got it, Mr. Tweed, sir. I got the Inspector and the saboteur. A statement, too. The one pilot is very chatty, but I think we need to talk to the woman. I'm certain she knows more."

"Eddie, this is Miss. Wicker, Mr. Bennett's assistant." Morrie gave the introductions. "Eddie is keen on becoming a reporter. Been hounding me for ages to take him on as a page. I thought today might be a good day to have him on payroll—just in case."

A knowing look passed between Louisa and Morrie. He'd suspected all along that the patent heist was a trap. He knew the syndicate would strike today and they might have to go incognito.

He'd built in a fail-safe along the way, *just in case.* Louisa marveled at the man standing before her. He claimed she'd saved his life, but really, he saved himself — she just set in motion the necessary events so he could help himself. His resourcefulness astounded her. *What must you have lived through to be this aware of the world?*

"It's time." Morrie inclined his head toward the center of the semi-circle where Elenore stood with Bennett. Bennett scanned the surrounding area, spotted her, and waved.

"Go on." Morrie nudged Louisa.

"What? Me? No. Today is their day. He's just being polite — waving hi."

"He's doing no such thing, Lou, and you know it."

She absently pushed the stray hairs back from her face. Louisa was in no fit state to be seen right now. Morrie must have guessed at the reason for hesitancy and turned her to face him.

"You are part of the team. He's calling you. Don't disappoint him." He plucked the cap from his head and placed it on Louisa's, smoothing the stray curls up underneath with gentle strokes. Her skin tingled well after he rotated her toward the stage and nudged her forward.

All eyes stared at her as she walked out to join Bennett and Elenore before the crowd. She glanced up at the glass box surrounded by guards in bright red and gold. Queen Victoria gazed down on her — on them. Louisa found the Judge, Viscount Fitzhugh, grinning smugly from a front-row seat, knowing that his minions had created enough havoc today to nullify Bennett's chances of verifying his patent and the solution to the drought.

But, as Bennett winked at Louisa and Elenore, and turned to address those assembled, a deep rumble vibrated the air and crackled in the now dense, dark clouds above.

Everyone looked up.

And the heavens poured.

* * *

THE LONDON CHRONICLE

From Thursday, November 2,
to Sunday, November 5, 1876

MONUMENTAL MAELSTROM
By Morrison Tweed

The talk of the town has got to be the engineering marvel of the year. On the afternoon of Saturday, November 4, Mr. Andrew Bennett submitted a final cloud seeding presentation to the Society of Engineers at the western base of London's Sky Port. The incredible thing—he made it rain.

While official approval of the patent will take a week to process, Her Majesty Queen Victoria gave the unofficial nod of approval when the skies opened and a torrent of ground-drenching rain followed.

Gerald Sterling, Mr. Bennett's closest competitor, still maintains his version of a cloud seeding patent is more sustainable. However, seeing as he has yet to put forward a request for a final presentation, one can only wonder when it might produce solid results.

In addition to the frenzy of the day, the London constabulary caught two criminals connected with the recent string of thefts and damage surrounding various entrepreneurs. Inspector Hersh has confirmed that the suspects in custody were caught red-handed.

The thief dubbed "Bug" by Shadow Phoenix set fire to the lead airship in the presentation convoy, and the one dubbed "Scythe" was caught prematurely deploying dispersal orbs during the flight's demonstration. However, Inspector Hersh remains mum regarding Shadow Phoenix and any involvement she may have had concerning their crimes over the past two months.

We look forward to an end to the drought and an announcement by the Society of Engineers welcoming Mr. Andrew Bennett into their fold.

Reviews are Golden

I would love to hear from you!
Please consider leaving a review on your
favourite social media platform, Amazon, or
Goodreads.

Reviews mean the world to authors.
Not only do we enjoy reading how you felt
about the book, but they help other readers get
a feel for a book in advance, and aid authors in
marketing.

Thank you for coming on this adventure with
me.

MJ

About the Author

Growing up in Ontario, Canada, **MJ Moores** was the only child of a single mom. MJ's passion for the arts ignited at a young age as she wrote adventure stories and read them aloud to close family and friends. The dramatic arts became a focus in high school as an aid to understanding character motivation in her writing. Majoring in Theatre Production at York University, with a minor in English, she went on to teach in both the elementary and high school divisions.

MJ currently lives with her husband and young son in Ontario, Canada. She keeps busy these days with her emerging authors' website Infinite Pathways, attending book fairs, and conferences as well as holding writing workshops and helping run the WCYR – Writers' Community of York Region.

mjmoores.com
facebook.com/AuthorMJMoores
twitter.com/AuthorMJMoores
goodreads.com/author/show/8104388.M_J_Moores